* * * * *

To Maureen

my wife, closest companion and dearest friend

* * * * *

Facts and Fantasies

Volume 4

a polished apple

Michael C. Cox

MIM

Mimast Inc

Mimast Inc

This paperback edition published in 2015 by Mimast Inc

Canadian ISBN 978-1-987926-03-3

All enquiries regarding this electronic edition to:

Mimast Inc
Edmonton
Alberta T6R 2H9
Canada
email: mimast@telus.net

Acknowledgements

Firstly, I must acknowledge a debt to the teachers who taught English language and English literature in my first five years at a Grammar school in my home town of Bristol. In spite of their efforts and best intentions, by the time I was sixteen I had acquired a taste for reading but not for writing. To be fair to those teachers, I felt at the time that I had so much to read and so little to write about.

I must acknowledge two of those teachers: Alex Mair, a Scotsman no less, and A.B. Reynolds, a somewhat eccentric Englishman. The former opened my eyes to literature by telling me to read Great Expectations by Charles Dickens. The latter opened my eyes to language by telling me to read out loud the first sentence in an exercise on syntax error: "Do not kill your wife with work, let electricity do it."

Secondly, I must thank my dear friend, Leif G. Stolee. He has encouraged me to write about people and events that have enriched my life over the past few decades. Leif's enthusiastic response to my stories has kept me at my computer and out of mischief. And I must mention here, James Stolee. He tempered his brother's enthusiasm with many well deserved criticisms of my writings.

Lastly but certainly not least, I must thank my wife, Maureen. She has always been my dearest and closest friend. She has watched over my grammar, corrected my spelling and made many constructive suggestions. Without Maureen's love and support, I doubt that I could ever have written a single word.

* * * * *

Needless to say, any mistakes in grammar and spelling, and any errors in facts used fictitiously, are my fault entirely. Nobody else is to blame.

* * * * *

THE FOUR STORIES

* * * * *

* * * * *

Author's note

These four short stories combine factual episodes and figments of my imagination in varied proportions. I have tried accurately to reveal the facts underlying all four stories but my memory is not what it was. In three of the stories, I have also tried to conceal the identities of the people involved. If I failed in the latter and thereby upset any family members, friends, colleagues or acquaintances, may I point out I never intended to embarrass and, more often than not, the law seems to benefit lawyers rather than litigants.

* * * * *

THE APPLE CART

The small retailer has not yet been entirely driven to the wall by the supermarket chain. Some have survived as street traders in open markets which have become popular tourist attractions, e.g. Petticoat Lane in London and Albert Cuypstraat in Amsterdam. In our house here in Canada we still have knick-knacks from flea markets as far afield as the Canary Islands, France and Mexico. This story was conceived as a small tribute to the many stall owners we have encountered around the world. As my research and writing of it proceeded, this story became more importantly a tribute to my Canadian friends and SEARIC - their charitable Society for the Education and Assistance of Rural Indian Children.

* * * * *

The day began like any other Friday. Kavi Cheema switched off the alarm just before it could go off at 3 a.m. In front of the wall mirror above the hand washbasin in his bedroom he carefully trimmed his already close-cropped beard before he showered in the tiny cubicle in the corner. In the kitchen he had a breakfast of orange juice and Muesli (a breakfast cereal of wheat flakes, toasted oats, fruit and nuts) over which he poured some milk.

In the hallway he pulled on his overalls, tied his shoe-laces and put on his woollen hat and gloves. In his father's old Ford minivan he checked the shopping list on his clip-board, started the engine, checked the blind spot over his right shoulder and moved off. Kavi was a proud member of the Institute of Advanced Motorists and strove to maintain its high standards of driving. He arrived safely at 'London's Larder' just after 4 a.m. without breaking any speed limits or contravening any road traffic acts.

New Covent Garden Market, set up in 1961 on the site of the old locomotive works at Nine Elms, is the wholesale food & flower market controlled by the government. Kavi collected what his father would have needed from the companies he had dealt with regularly. As always, just like his father did, he left the apples until last. As always, he took his time to inspect each individual apple. He had become immune to the supplier's banter about his father's minivan.

'Old 'enry Ford made it 'ere then, Kev!' In the market everybody called him Kevin or Kev – never Kavi.

'Nah,' replied Kavi, mimicking their London Cockney accents, 'Ee packed up at Battersea an' I 'ad ter shove 'im the rest of the way 'ere, cor blimey.'

Kavi gave time for the laughter to die down then headed for Old 'enry Ford.

He was back in Southall and able to unload the van at his father's stall in The Broadway before 6 a.m. If the traffic warden caught him unloading after 6 a.m., when restrictions applied, he'd face a parking fine – known in law as a fixed penalty or penalty charge. Kavi knew it was not a criminal matter but in his position he could not afford even to break a local authority traffic regulation.

It was just after half past six when he parked Old 'enry Ford outside his parents' terraced house in Oswald Road and put the resident's permit on the dashboard. When he opened the front door Kavi heard the Panjabi radio broadcast coming from the kitchen. His mother was up. She was probably getting breakfast ready for Rajender, his 11 year old son who was just coming down the stairs. He was in his pyjamas.

Raj had been woken up by the noise of the minivan pulling up outside the house. Kavi still could not get used to the rattle of the engine and the squealing brakes. 'The BMW 5 series saloon, or any BMW car for that matter, would never make this noise,' he thought, as he slammed the driver's door three times before it finally shut.

'Kavi sat sree akaal,' said Mrs. Cheema as she poured glasses of orange juice for her son and grandson.

'Ma sat sree akaal,' he replied in Panjabi to his mother before saying in English to his son 'Good morning, Raj.'

'Hi, Dad,' his son replied in English with the slightest hint of a French accent.

'When is your maths test today?'

'First thing this morning.'

'Good luck. Come to the stall after school. You can give me a hand and tell me how you got on. OK?'

'OK, Dad,'

'Here's an apple for your teacher but don't give it to her until you've got your test result. I don't want to defend you against bribery and corruption charges.'

Kavi walked up Oswald Road to The Broadway to prepare the family stall for business just as his father used to do. 'Display all our fruit and vegetables so our customers can see what they are buying,' his father would say. Kavi did just that. He took extra care with the apples. Each one was individually polished before being arranged into a tall pyramid on a little wooden handcart at the front of the stall.

The cart belonged to Kavi's father who used it to sell fruit and vegetables door to door when he first came to England. When they opened their business in the Broadway, his father named the stall 'The Apple Cart' and kept his little handcart at the front as a reminder of their humble beginnings.

'Everything must be tip top and fair price,' his father insisted. 'Always be friendly and polite so the customers will be coming back again and again.' When Kavi's father died, many of his customers came to pay their respects and offer their condolences. Kavi often recalled his father's story about a Brahmin, who had an infinite supply of something that was absolutely worthless until he gave it away.

'What was it that the Brahmin had?' Kavi's father would ask. When Kavi pretended he didn't know, his father would smile and say, 'Kavi, the Brahmin had what I am just giving to you. You are receiving smile. Remember, Kavi, to be giving everybody smiles.'

* * * * *

When Kavi opened the stall at 7:30 a.m. he smiled at his first customer. As he was serving her, a small group of pupils from Beaconsfield School sauntered up and stood close to the apple cart. He was handing the lady her change when the group turned and ran as the pyramid started to collapse. Apples were falling off the cart and bouncing in every direction.

It happened so quickly. One minute there was a pyramid of polished apples. A moment later much of the fruit was lying bruised or broken on the floor. The worst of it was that Kavi saw his son, Raj, in the group running down the road. And he had an apple in his hand.

That Friday afternoon Kavi closed the stall early and at 3 o'clock marched down Oswald Street to Beaconsfield School. He was standing in the foyer when the bell signalled the end of school. 'There's yer dad by the door,' said Adil, 'and 'e don't look 'appy.' As soon as he saw him, Raj guessed his father was all out of smiles.

'Hi Dad!'

'Who are these boys?' asked Kavi.

'Adil, Sunil and Vijay. They're my friends.'

'Which one of you upset my apples this morning?' asked Kavi, glaring at the three boys.

Kavi hadn't actually seen Raj take the apple from the cart but he had seen him running away with an apple in his hand.

11

'Circumstantial evidence - two or more facts taken together to infer a conclusion about something unknown,' Kavi reminded himself.

'They didn't do it, Dad. I did. It was an accident.'

'What do you mean, it was an accident?'

'We dared 'im.' said Adil. 'We told 'im 'e 'ad to pinch an apple if 'e wanted to be in our gang. Vijay told 'im which one to pinch.'

'Vijay told 'im to grab the corner apple at the bottom. We didn't fink them apples would fall off the cart,' lied Sunil.

'We are very sorry, Mr. Cheema,' said Vijay.

'You don't look sorry, any of you.' said Kavi. 'Take those silly grins off your faces.'

'I'm sorry, Dad. I didn't think.'

'That's your trouble,' said Kavi, 'you don't always think. Those apples will come out of your pocket money. Let's go home.'

At that moment, Raj's class teacher appeared. 'Good afternoon Miss Kumar,' the boys chorused.

'Good afternoon Raj, Adil, Sunil, Vijay,' she said, smiling back at them. The attractive, dark-haired young teacher then looked at Kavi. 'Good afternoon! Mr. Cheema, is it?'

'Yes. Kavi Cheema. Good afternoon Miss Kumar,' he said, giving her his broadest smile.

'Will you be coming to the parents' evening next week?'

'Ah, yes, the parents' evening. Next week. I think so. Goodness me. Yes. Yes.'

'Good!' she said, 'It's our first meeting of the school year and the first chance for me to meet the parents of my pupils. I look forward to seeing you there, Mr. Cheema.' She smiled, this time at Kavi, and headed for the staff room.

Raj saw his dad's smile vanish as soon as Miss Kumar was out of sight. First the apples. Now he was in trouble for losing his teacher's letter about parents' evening. To make matters worse, he didn't think he had done his best in the maths test that morning.

As they walked home side by side, Kavi recalled how it had been when he misbehaved and let his father down. He remembered how his father forgave him especially when he owned up right away and didn't try to put the blame on somebody else. 'Kavi,' he would say, 'you are being foolish boy but I forgive you because you owned up and were sorry.'

'Rajender!'

'Yes Dad!'

'Why didn't I know there was a parents' evening next week?'

'It's my fault, Dad. I forgot to bring home the letter. I'm sorry. I just forgot.'

'I felt foolish when your teacher asked me if I was coming.'

'Sorry, Dad.'

'Well, alright. I forgive you. Don't forget again.'

'No, Dad.'

'Now about those apples... '

'Yes, Dad.'

'If I tell you how many were ruined, how much each apple cost me and how much a customer would have paid me for one, can you work out how many weeks it will take you to repay me if I deduct half your weekly pocket money?'

'Yes, Dad.'

* * * * *

13

Deeptikana Kumar was glad to sit down. It was the end of her fifth week in her first term in her first full-time teaching post. In front of her, on the small table in the corner, were the papers from the maths test that morning. Most of the teachers had already gone home. She had the staff room to herself. Correcting and marking her pupils' work was not her favourite occupation but it had to be done. What would her colleagues think if she didn't do any marking? She had yet to discover the value of what psychologists call immediate feedback.

Mrs. Frobisher, due to retire at the end of term, all too frequently commanded her pupils to change papers and mark one another's test. 'Strike while the iron is hot and make them learn from each other's mistakes,' the formidable lady would bark to justify her stratagem but never, of course, admitting that re-marking took much less of her time than marking!

Deeptikana entered the scores in her mark book and compared them with those of the two earlier tests. There were no surprises. Adil, Sunil and Vijay were near the bottom of the class and Rajender Cheema, her star pupil, was again top and the only one with full marks. Remembering her encounter with the four boys in the school entrance, she wondered why Mr. Cheema's clever son associated with those three mischievous, not-so-clever imps.' Perhaps she could broach the subject at the parents' evening. 'What,' she thought to herself, 'was Mr. Cheema saying to those boys this afternoon?'

'You are late, Deeptikana.'

'Sorry, Dad. I had a test to mark.'

'Please do not call me Dad.'

'Sorry, Father.'

'Your mother is just putting the food on the table.'

'Tell Mum I shall be there in a moment.'

'Please do not refer to your mother as Mum.'

Mr. Kumar sat with his head bowed and his eyes closed while Mrs. Kumar served first him and then her daughter. When she had

14

served herself, she looked at her husband and then, shaking her head, glanced at her daughter. Prathamesh Kumar opened his eyes and without looking up he began to eat.

'So, Father - how was your day?'

'Please do not be bothering your father, Deep. We are having very bad day.'

'Is it Amal again?'

'No. It is not your brother.'

'It is problem with business. Please be eating your food, Deep.'

'Where is Amal anyway? Is he working late at the office again?'

'Amalesh is at the office where he should be,' said Mr. Kumar, looking up from his plate.

'What is he doing there, Father? What is wrong?'

'It is not your concern. Finish your food and help your mother in the kitchen.'

As her daughter loaded the dishwasher, Mrs. Ravinder Kumar put on her bright yellow kitchen gloves and started to wash up the pots and pans. When her father retreated into his study at the front of their large house, Deeptikana broke the silence and asked her mother what was bothering her father.

* * * * *

Prathamesh Kumar inherited the East India Woollen & Silk Carpets Ltd import business from his father, Parmesh. Had he bothered, Pramathesh could have traced his roots to Bhadohi in Uttar Pradesh. Located almost 300 feet above sea level, it is one of the oldest and largest carpet manufacturing districts in India.

His great-great-grandfather, Varesh Kumar, had been a master weaver in Bhadohi. His great-grandfather, Deepak Kumar, had learned the craft of hand-knotted carpets from his father, Varesh.

15

Prathamesh's grandfather, Mahesh Kumar, had also become a master weaver in Bhadohi but he was not content just to weave someone else's carpets. He wanted his own business. So, through prudence, sheer hard work and the help of his three sons, Gagnesh, Parmesh and Bhuvanesh, he established his own workshop to produce carpets of only the highest quality.

When Britain declared war on Germany in 1939, Gagnesh, the eldest son, left his father's business to serve as a captain in the Army of India. He died fighting the Japanese in Burma. After the war, Parmesh came to England, married by arrangement the daughter of the owner of several large warehouses and became a British citizen.

When their father, Mahesh, died of a heart attack, Parmesh allowed Bhuvanesh, his younger brother, to take over the business in India and arranged for him to marry the daughter of a major carpet manufacturer in the nearby district of Mirzapur. Back in England, Parmesh formed the East India Woollen & Silk Carpets Ltd to import carpets from Uttar Pradesh.

When Prathamesh was born in Southall, Britain had already started down the road to post-war prosperity. Rationing was a thing of the past and people were beginning to buy their own homes. After India had proclaimed itself a republic in January 1950, thousands of Indians – many unskilled - came to Britain to find work especially in the Midlands. Pramesh wanted cheap flat weave carpets for these immigrants. 'Make as many dhurries as you can,' he told Bhuvanesh, 'and make them as cheaply and as quickly as possible.'

Pramesh's younger brother did as he was told. The loose weave, pile-less cotton and wool rugs became very popular in the Midlands. 'Make sure the dhurries are brightly coloured,' commanded Pramesh. 'These immigrants want something to cheer up their gloomy lives.' Again Bhuvanesh did as he was told. Why not? Pramesh was his elder brother and head of the family. And their export-import business was booming.

Almost as soon as he could walk, Prathamesh would go with his father to one or other of the warehouses. When he was a little older but still not at school, he would, if his father wasn't looking, sit astride a roll of carpet and pretend to be riding a horse. When he had

16

started school and was learning geometry, Prathamesh became fascinated by the two-fold symmetry of the designs in the expensive carpets his father had started to import. He liked the floral and vine patterns but preferred the animal, bird and calligraphic ones. Prathamesh was also intrigued by the different kinds of knots used in hand-made carpets.

'Weavers came to India in the 16th century and taught us how to make hand-knotted wool and silk carpets,' said his father. 'A Persian knot – also called a Senneh or Farsibaff – is an asymmetrical single knot; the thread forms one loop around one of the two warps. There are other knots, of course, but what matters is the knot density – the more knots per square inch (kpsi) the better the quality and the more expensive the carpet. Our best carpets have more than 300 kpsi,' said his father with pride.

One evening after he had finished his geometry homework, Prathamesh showed his father sketches of four possible knots.

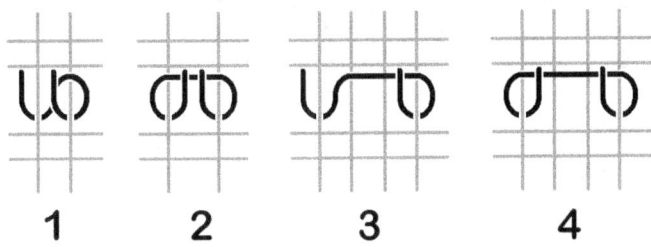

'Very good,' said Pramesh. 'Number 1 is a Persian knot. Number 2 is a Turkish knot. Numbers 3 and 4 are Jufti knots. Which Jufti is symmetrical?' Prathamesh was peeved that his father should even bother to ask him such a silly question but he just smiled, nodded and pointed to number 4. 'Well done,' said his father, not noticing the wry look on his son's face when he patted him on the shoulder.

Prathamesh joined his father's business after he had graduated and completed his articles to qualify as an accountant. He took over the company when his father, like grandfather Mahesh Kumar, died of a heart attack.

* * * * *

When Kavi and Raj arrived back at Oswald Road they were greeted by the sound of the radio and the smell of curry coming from the kitchen. Mrs. Cheema greeted them as usual. Raj said 'hello Gran' and ran upstairs before Kavi could reprimand him for not practising his Panjabi.

Kavi did not tell his mother what happened that morning. He knew it would upset her. Instead he told her that next week he would be going to the parents' evening at Beaconsfield School to see Raj's teacher and asked if she would like to go with him. She declined. She loved her grandson but accepted that she could never take the place of her late daughter-in-law. While his mother finished preparing the meal, Kavi sat in his father's old chair and looked at the advertisement he had placed in the local newspaper.

MANAGER WANTED
For 'The Apple Cart' Fruit & Vegetable Stall
in The Broadway, Southall
Must have current driving licence
Apply to Fosdyke, Cheema & Wong
tel: 020-7964-0469

When the food was ready, Kavi called Raj down from his bedroom to the table in the corner of the living room. Mrs. Cheema served her son and then her grandson before she sat down and served herself. 'Shukriya, Daddi,' Raj said to his grandmother. Kavi and his mother smiled at one another. 'That was right, wasn't it, Dad?'

Kavi nodded, thinking how lucky he was to have such a clever son who didn't say Dadda (grandfather) and remind his mother of her late husband. 'Can I help you at the stall tomorrow, Dad?' When Kavi frowned, Raj said, 'Sorry, Dad, may I help you tomorrow?' Kavi nodded and smiled at his son. He was indeed an intelligent boy.

Saturday came and went. They had sold out long before 5 o'clock. Raj handled the till all day while Kavi weighed and bagged the fruit and vegetables for the customers. Raj cashed up and filled in the bank paying-in slip. Kavi swept the floor and washed the counters. On the way back to Oswald Road Kavi paused outside the bank so that Raj could pay the day's takings into the overnight safe.

'You did well today, Raj. I was proud of you. How would you like to manage your grandfather's stall?' He laughed out loud when Raj replied, 'Just as much as you would like to, Dad.'

Kavi, much to his mother's disapproval, had decided not to open the stall on Mondays. Business was usually slow and Monday was the one day when he could pop into the city, specifically to The Square Mile. He left Old 'enry Ford parked at Southall station – one of only two railway stations in Britain where the name on the platform is in both the Latin alphabet and the Gurmukhī script.

The 9.15 arrived at Paddington on time. During the 14-minute journey Kavi managed to glance at his weekly Gazette of the Law Society. The London Underground was busy as usual so it was standing room only on the Bakerloo line to Oxford Circus and on the East-bound Central line to Chancery Lane.

When he stepped out of the underground station and crossed High Holborn into Chancery Lane, there was a nip in the air. Leaves on the trees at Lincoln's Inn were turning colour and beginning to fall in the bright autumn sunshine. As Kavi walked through the Gate House and along a path strewn with dead leaves, he heard in his mind's ear Marie Claire, his late wife, singing her favourite song - Les Feuilles Mortes.

She always sang Jacques Prevert's lyrics to Joseph Kosma's tune. 'Non! Never shall I sing those words,' she would shout when Kavi, pretending not to understand French, would start singing Johnny Mercer's lyrics for Autumn Leaves. When he reached the refrain she would sing loudly in French to drown out the English.

Kavi would stop singing and laugh. Then he would hold her in his arms and whisper gently: 'Je t'aime beaucoup, Marie Claire. Je t'aimerai toujours.'

It was almost four years since a drunk driver ran over her on a pedestrian crossing but to Kavi it still seemed like yesterday. As he approached the four-storey building, a gust of wind swept away the dead leaves - les feuilles mortes - on the stone steps leading to the chambers of William S. Fosdyke, QC. and he recalled Johnny Mercer's final words of the refrain. Kavi did miss his darling Marie Claire most of all when the autumn leaves started to fall.

'Good morning, Bill.'

'Namastay, Kavi.'

'Nice try, Bill, but that's Hindi not Panjabi. Here's a present for you.'

'An apple?'

'Well spotted, counsellor. I hope our clients appreciate your razor sharp mind.'

'Is it from The Apple Cart?'

'Actually it's from New Covent Garden.'

'Is it fresh?'

'It all depends upon what we mean by fresh. May I respectfully refer you to the case of Jones v. Smith and the deep-frozen, smoked kipper hermetically sealed in plastic. Your Honour, I contend that my client had every right to ask if the kipper was fresh and that my client should not have been subjected to public ridicule.'

'Allow me to rephrase the question. On what day and at what time did learned counsel acquire said apple from New Covent Garden?'

'Last Friday morning at approximately 4.25 a.m.'

'I'm grateful to my learned colleague.'

'My pleasure. You realise I have just treated you to lunch?

'Lunch?'

'Yes. You know what they say? An apple a day...'

'keeps the judges at bay?'

'So, Bill, you wanted to see me?'

* * * * *

Mrs. Kumar finished the pots and pans, took off her yellow washing up gloves and led Deep into the sewing room at the back of the house. Before she sat down in her favourite chair - by the French windows that led to their large garden - Mrs. Kumar offered to make some tea but Deep knew her mother was stalling. She took a seat facing her mother and asked again what was troubling her father. Reluctantly, Mrs. Kumar sat down and tried to explain.

'Your father is worrying about business.'

'What has Amal been doing now to upset Dad?'

'Nothing. He is doing nothing.'

'That's what he usually does.'

'No, no. Amalesh is working hard.'

'So what has he been doing wrong?'

'Nothing. He is doing nothing wrong.'

'So what is Dad worrying about? Is he still upset because I teach and don't work for him in our family business?'

'No. Your father is very proud of you being good teacher.'

'So what is he worrying about?'

21

Deep's mother sighed. Just as she was about to answer, Deep frowned and looked towards the door thinking she had heard the sound of her father's study door opening. Her mother appeared to have heard nothing. She started to answer her daughter's question.

'It is your father's uncle, Bhuvanesh.'

'What has he been doing?'

'He is saying that he is doing what his brother, Pramesh, told him to do.'

'What did grandfather tell him to do?'

'He is saying that your grandfather was telling him to use children to make carpets.'

'Does he use child labour? Does Dad know he uses children to make carpets?'

'How can you be asking me such a thing, Deep?'

Before either of them could say any more, the door opened and Deep's father came in.

'Father! You don't look very well. Please come and sit down.'

'No thank you. I am very tired. I came to say goodnight. I am going to bed.'

The next morning Deep knocked on her brother's bedroom door and went in. Amal was still asleep. He looked so awful that she crept out, closed the door behind her and went down to breakfast. Her mother was already in the garden. She guessed her father was working in his study. She did not disturb him. She had her week's lessons to prepare so she worked at the kitchen table and waited for her brother.

Amal eventually appeared in his pyjamas and dressing gown. Deep noticed he was wearing the slippers she gave him for his birthday. She cleared a space on the table and put down a mug of coffee. Her brother yawned and flopped onto the kitchen chair opposite her. Before he had taken a sip of the hot black coffee she asked him what was going on.

'What d'you mean, what's going on?'

'This trouble with Dad's uncle?'

'Oh, that! I thought you meant...'

'Thought I meant what?'

'You know, the same old thing. Dad doesn't think I work hard enough.'

'Well perhaps you don't. He knows you'd rather be doing something else.'

'I would. I hate the warehouse and I'm sick of all those carpets.'

'Why didn't you come home for supper last night?'

'I was busy.'

'At the warehouse?'

'Yes, as a matter of fact.'

'What were you doing? Fiddling the cash book?'

'No. Never. Dad would spot it in a minute. You know what he's like with figures.'

'So you'd fiddle the books if you could get away with it?'

'You know I wouldn't. I do have some scruples. I'm a man of integrity.'

'So what were you doing at the warehouse.'

'Can you keep a secret?'

'Depends what it is?'

'I was applying for a management job in Southall.'

'Dad won't be pleased. That will be something else for him to worry about.'

'So what's old Bhuv been up to? Breaking the law?'

'It's possible. He may have been using illegal child labour to weave those carpets you import to keep us in the lap of luxury.'

* * * * *

Mandy, assistant to the Clerk of Chambers, teetered on her high heels into Bill Fosdyke's room carrying a silver tray on which was a pot of coffee, a jug of cream, two cups, two saucers, some sachets of sweetener and several chocolate biscuits. When she had teetered out and closed the door, Bill poured two coffees and selected a biscuit. Kavi refused cream and sweetener but accepted a biscuit. Black coffee and dark chocolate biscuits still reminded him of his days at Oxford. 'What,' asked Bill, raising his cup to his lips, 'do you know about child labour in India?'

'According to Section 24 of The Constitution of India (which came into force on the 26th January 1950) - Prohibition of employment of children in factories, etc.:

No child below the age of fourteen years shall be employed to work in any factory or mine or engaged in any other hazardous employment.

The Child Labour (Prohibition & Regulation) Act of 1986 broadened the scope of the ban on child employment by introducing

fines from 10,000 to 20,000 rupees per child employed and prison term penalties of up to two years.

In October 2006 the 1986 Act was amended to include a

ban on employing children under fourteen years of age as domestic workers or servants, in dhabas, restaurants, hotels, motels, tea-shops, spas and other recreational centres.'

'What are dhabas?'

'Road-side eateries,' said Kavi. 'Definitely not places for a gourmet such as yourself.'

'Are these laws enforced?'

'Not very effectively. There are few government inspectors with too much ground to cover to eradicate this age-old social evil as the Gazette of India Extraordinary called it.'

'How do you happen to know so much about this?'

'Marie Claire. She kept on to me to do something. "Kavi," she'd say, "you must stop these parents selling their children into bonded labour." I confess to my shame that I couldn't see that there was anything I could do. Anyway, what's brought all this on?'

'A client. He's been importing carpets from his uncle who is being charged with, among other things, trafficking of children, illegal use of child bonded labour and exporting carpets without a proper customs & excise licence. He came to see me on Friday. Has our client good reason to be worried?'

'His uncle might well have. What's his name?'

'The uncle?'

'The client.'

'Kumar. Prathamesh Kumar,' said Bill checking his notes. 'Name ring a bell?'

'A faint one perhaps but Kumar is the Indian equivalent of Smith. Rajender's teacher is a Kumar. Very attractive and intelligent to boot. Actually I shall be seeing her on Wednesday evening.'

'I see,' said Bill with a knowing look.

'You don't see at all. It's the school's parents' evening – the first this term. Anyway, it's time I was off.'

'Oh, I nearly forgot. Mandy took a phone call this morning. Someone's after your job.'

'My job?'

'Manager of The Apple Cart,' said Bill smiling and taking a bite out of his free lunch.

On his way to the Clerk's office, Kavi paused at an open doorway. David Wong looked up from his desk and asked when he should file bankruptcy papers for The Apple Cart. His grin turned to a look of alarm as a large orange flew at him. 'Well caught,' said Kavi to his squash opponent. 'I see you're keeping in shape ready for our next encounter – whenever that might be,' he said over his shoulder as he hurried down the corridor.

He knocked and opened the door just inside the main entrance to Chambers. 'Message for me, Mandy?' She nodded and told him that a Mr. Kumar had telephoned to apply for the job of manager of The Apple Cart. 'Not another Kumar! That's the fourth today,' said Kavi. A puzzled Mandy shook her head, consulted her notepad and told him that only one person had so far enquired about the position. He laid his broadest smile on her. 'Please telephone this Mr. Kumar and instruct him to be at the stall in The Broadway this Thursday afternoon - to meet the owner of The Apple Cart – at four o'clock sharp.'

* * * * *

Miss Kumar was sitting at her uncluttered desk when Kavi arrived at the open classroom door five minutes before his 7.15 p.m. appointment. He apologised for being early and asked if he might look around the room and see his son's desk. She nodded, smiled and pointed to the group of four desks near the fish tank.

A card, on which Raj had neatly printed his name, marked his son's desk. The other cards showed the other three desks belonged to another boy and two girls. Raj's desk was neat and tidy. Inside were some notebooks. In one of them Raj had started an essay entitled 'Upsetting The Apple Cart'. Kavi was starting to read it when he heard Miss Kumar inviting him to sit down.

26

'I'm sorry,' she said as he lowered himself onto the chair, 'these seats are not very comfortable or suitable for someone who is six feet tall.'

'Six feet three inches, actually, but please don't apologise. I've experienced worse.'

'Mr. Cheema, I must tell you that you have a very intelligent and very hard-working son.'

'That's good to hear, Miss Kumar.'

'In fact, Mr. Cheema, Rajender is my star pupil.'

'I hope you're not saying that because he bribes you with apples.'

'No, of course not,' she said with a puzzled look on her face.

'Just my little joke, Miss Kumar. Please forgive me. How did Raj do in his maths test?'

'Full marks. That's full marks for three tests in a row now.'

'What about his other subjects?'

'Again, he is usually top of the class.'

'And how are his social skills? That is the current jargon I believe.'

'Ah, I'm glad you asked that. Actually I'm a little worried by his choice of friends.'

'You mean Adil, Sunil and Vijay? I notice that you have seated them well apart from one another in the classroom.'

'Yes I have,' said Deeptikana, surprised that Kavi had remembered their names and had noticed they weren't sitting near one another. 'They get up to all sorts of tricks when they are together.'

27

'Boys will be boys, is that not so?'

'According to the headmaster of Narkover School.'

'Doctor Alec Smart – played by Will Hay - in the 1935 British mystery film entitled...'

'Boys will be boys,' said Deeptikana, glancing at her watch. 'I wonder why we never say girls will be girls.'

Hearing footsteps outside the classroom door and suspecting that the interview was nearly over, Kavi stood up and held out his hand. 'Thank you for seeing me. My son is fortunate to have you as his teacher.'

'I wish all my pupils were like Raj, Mr. Cheema.'

'Might that not be rather boring for you?'

'It might, Mr. Cheema. It just might be.'

'Before I go, Miss Kumar, I should like to ask you two questions if you have a moment.'

'Certainly,' she said.

'Did my son give you an apple before or after you marked his latest maths test?'

'Actually it was after. I remember it well. When everybody had left the classroom, he put the apple on my desk and said, "Cette pomme est pour vous, mademoiselle. Bon appétit." I had no idea he spoke French.'

'His mother was French. You might say that French is his mother tongue. However, his mother always claimed she was Parisienne rather than Française.'

'And your second question?'

'Would you consider it bribery and corruption if I invited you to have dinner with me on Saturday evening at my favourite restaurant?'

'No, not at all,' was all she said with a quizzical look on her face.

'Perhaps I should rephrase the question. Would you dine with me this Saturday evening?'

'Thank you, Mr. Cheema. I should like that very much.'

'Then I shall call for you at 7.15 p.m. if I may.' said Kavi giving her a broad smile.

* * * * *

Amal jumped when the phone rang on his desk in the corner of the warehouse. His father was in a foul mood and had just taken it out on his son. 'Hello,' said Amal. He completely forgot his father's instructions always to say Good afternoon. East India Woollen & Silk Carpet Import Company. How may I help you? The voice at the other end of the phone asked for Mr. Kumar.

'I'm Amalesh Kumar. Who is this please?' When he heard that it was Miss Amanda Winters of Fosdyke, Cheema & Wong, Barristers at Law, he held the phone closer to his ear and looked nervously around to see where his father was. On the other end of the line Mandy passed on the instructions for Amal to write down on his telephone notepad. 'This Thursday. O.K. 4 o'clock sharp at the stall. O.K. In The Broadway. O.K. I understand. Thank you. I'll be there.'

Raj gave the customer her change while Kavi put the two bags of fruit and vegetables into her wheel-along trolley. It was now 3.55 p.m. The only customer left was a young man dressed in a dark suit, white shirt and silk tie. His black leather shoes were highly polished.

Raj smiled. 'Good afternoon, Sir, what would you like?' Amalesh, clearing his throat, explained that he had come about the position of manager and believed that he was to meet the owner of

The Apple Cart here at 4 o'clock. 'Dad! There's a man here to see the owner of this stall.'

Kavi emerged from behind some crates. 'And who might you be, young man?'

'Kumar. Amalesh Kumar. I have applied for the position of manager.'

'Ah! I see you're on time. One minute late and you would have been too late. You've passed the first test. So far so good.'

'Thank you, Sir. I am sorry but I do not know your name.'

'For now you can just call me Sir. Here's your next test. Serve this customer.'

'Excuse me?'

'Find out what Mrs. Joshi wants and serve her.'

'Very well,' said Amal. And with that he went up to the elderly lady, gave her a big smile and said, 'Good afternoon, Mrs. Joshi. How are you today?' When she gave him a puzzled look, he smiled again and said, 'Namastay, Smt. Joshi. Aap kaise hain?'

Raj gave Mrs. Joshi her change while Amal carefully put her fruit in a double bag.

'Excellent. You passed test number 2. Here's the third one. Help Raj close up the stall. He'll tell you what to do.'

None of this was what Amal had expected. He was enjoying himself. He removed his tie, took off his coat, rolled up his shirt sleeves and did what he was told. Sweep the floor. Wipe over the counters. Cover the unsold fruit and vegetables. Stack the empty crates. Count the cash in the till and record the exact details in the daily ledger. Pull down the shutters and secure with the padlocks. After he had secured the last padlock, Amal did up the buttons on his shirt sleeves and put back on his coat and tie.

'Did Mr. Kumar pass the test number 3, Raj?'

'Yes, Dad, he did.'

'Congratulations, Mr. Kumar. Just two more tests to go. Follow me to our headquarters.'

'Is that where my formal interview with the owner will take place, Sir?'

'Yes, I suppose so. Yes, if you pass test number 4,' said Kavi winking at his son.

* * * * *

With two chairs, his desk and the surrounding floor strewn with documents, Bill Fosdyke looked far from his usually unruffled self when David Wong arrived carrying his orange. Clearing a chair, David sat down. Bill took a bite from his apple and handed over a copy of The Children (Pledging of Labour) Act, 1933. David managed to read the note Bill had written on the cover page.

Raj (Hindi for reign) = British occupation and rule of India. Act banned all agreements whereby parents or guardians could receive payments or benefits in kind from employers for allowing any children below 15 (now 14) years of age to be used in any employment.

'We need Kavi's input on this,' said David. 'When's he returning to the fold?'

'Soon, very soon, I hope. Apparently, Marie Claire, kept India's child labour problem under his nose the whole time.'

'A lovely lady. Such a sad loss.'

'Yes she was. I think Kavi will want to be in on this one for her sake.'

'What did Kavi have to say on our client's behalf this morning?'

'He thinks our client's uncle – the one in India – could be in big trouble. But as for our client, we need to know more about his business relationship with his uncle.'

'D'you want me to look into that?'

'Would you mind?'

'No sooner said that done,' said David as he began to peel his orange.

'I gather from the orange in your hand that Kavi looked in on you this morning.'

'Nearly knocked my block off,' said David. 'He did not, I trust, throw that apple at you.' 'Certainly not. Unlike some I could mention, Mr. Cheema has proper respect for Head of Chambers. Now be about your business. Lunch is over,' said Bill dropping the apple core into his waste basket.

* * * * *

Kavi, Raj and Amal walked in the direction of the High Street, crossed over The Broadway and then turned into Oswald Road. When they reached Old 'enry Ford, Kavi asked to see Amal's driving licence. Satisfied that it did not restrict the holder to an automatic car, he gave Amal the keys of the minivan and told him his next test was to take them for a drive. 'What next?' Amal asked himself, as he drove them around the block and through the heavy homecoming traffic along the Broadway.

Just after they had passed it, Kavi asked him to explain the traffic sign close to their stall. Amal had no idea. Amal hadn't even noticed the sign. He was having a great time driving this old minivan around town. And he couldn't believe its colours: orange, pea-green and pineapple. It was like driving around in a bowl of fruit salad. His father would have been mortified. Cool! Real cool!

Back at Oswald Road, Amal parked the van, put the resident's permit back on the dashboard and managed to close the driver's door first time without slamming it. Kavi was impressed. 'You should consider taking an advanced motoring course, Mr. Kumar. I believe you would enjoy it? Incidentally, that road sign you missed gives the loading & unloading restrictions relating to the section of road and kerb marked by yellow lines. Now for the test number 5. Come and meet my mother. She speaks Hindi as well as Panjabi. By the way, you may now call me Mr. Cheema.'

Inside the house Amal heard the Panjabi broadcast coming from Mrs. Cheema's portable radio and savoured the aroma from the chicken kourma in the pot on the table in the corner of the room. He noticed that Kavi's mother had already set four places. Amal greeted Mrs. Cheema politely in Hindi and introduced himself. She smiled – first at Amal and then at Kavi. When they were all seated and tucking into the food, Raj asked Amal what he did for a living. 'In Hindi if you please,' said Kavi.

He began by telling them that he worked for his father as so-called manager of a carpet warehouse but that he was really just a general factotum: answer the phone, make the tea, sweep the floor and generally keep the place tidy. Kavi smiled to himself and refrained from pointing out that general is redundant because factotum means a person employed to do all kinds of work.

Realising that he wasn't helping his case, Amal tried to redress the balance by saying that, on reflection, he was more than just a dog's-body. In his father's company he was responsible for checking and recording the delivery and dispatch of the carpets, keeping the day-to-day accounts, making up the weekly wage packets and controlling the petty cash. Raj wanted to know why Amal would want to run a fruit and vegetable stall but at that point he asked him, 'Do you love your father?'

'Oh! Nobody's asked me that before. You know what, I've never asked myself that. I often hate the way he treats me. Do this. Do that. Hurry up. Never please do this, Amal. Please do that, Amal. Thank you, Amal. And it's always Amalesh. Never Amal.'

'That's too bad,' said Raj, with a look that said my dad's not like that.

'Hey, and I always have to say Father. He gets really mad if I say Dad.'

'Perhaps,' said Kavi, 'your father thinks you're disrespectful by calling him Dad.'

'I hadn't thought of it that way, Mr. Cheema,' said Amal. 'My father's a brilliant man, you know. He's got a degree. He's a Fellow of the Institute of Chartered Accountants.'

'Do you like your dad?' said Raj.

'No. Yes. No, I don't always like,' said Amal, 'but I admire and respect him, I guess.'

'So why not stay in the family business?' asked Kavi.

'I want to make it on my own. And I'll never be able to fill Dad's shoes.'

'Do you live at home with your parents?'

'Yes, Mrs. Cheema, I do. I always have done.'

'The Manager of The Apple Cart would be required to live here. Board and lodgings would be part of the salary,' said Kavi. 'How would you feel about that?'

'Cool,' thought Amal but said aloud, 'that would be most acceptable, Mr. Cheema. When do I meet the owner for my formal interview, if I may ask?'

'You've met him,' said Kavi, 'and you've had it.'

When they saw the look on Amal's face, Mrs. Cheema and Raj started laughing.

'The job is yours if you want it,' said Kavi.

'Thank you,' said Amal, beaming broadly. 'Thank you so much. When do I start?'

'As soon as possible.'

* * * * *

Deep and Amal broke their news to their father on Saturday morning when they thought he was in a receptive frame of mind. They had told their mother earlier – Deep on Wednesday evening and Amal on Thursday evening. Amal was first to speak to his father. He was surprised, even a little hurt (he admitted to himself) but delighted that his dad didn't get angry. 'When do you take up your appointment?'

Amal told him it would be a week on Monday. 'Very well,' said his father, 'I shall promote Mukharjee and you will have a week to show him the ropes.' Amal told him that it was a live-in position but did not tell him where he would be working and living. His father did not seem to care. When Deep broke her news, she got an entirely different reaction.

'Who is this person you will be seeing this evening? What is his name and what does he do?'

'He is the parent of one of my pupils.'

'A married man! You are seeing a married man?'

When Amal heard this, he made a hurried escape to his room upstairs.

'No, Father, he is a widower. His wife died four years ago.'

'What does he do, this widower?'

'He sells fruit and vegetables.'

'He is a greengrocer! You know he is a greengrocer and you want to sit down and eat with him? No. I forbid it. The daughter of a merchant cannot eat with a greengrocer.'

'Father, we are British citizens living in England. The caste system doesn't apply here.'

'I am your father. I forbid this.'

'Father, listen. I do not wish to be disrespectful but the time is long past when Gandhi had to ask the Modh Bania permission to leave India to study law in England.'

'You know what Bania means?'

'Yes, Father, I know. Merchant. And Gandhi means greengrocer in Hindi. I know.'

'Prathamesh,' said Deep's mother, 'please be giving your daughter your permission.'

'I'm sorry, Mother, but I do not need his permission. I should like it,' she said, 'but I do not need it,' and flounced out of the room.

Turning to his wife, he raised his voice and asked, 'What is this greengrocer's name?'

'Mr. Kavi Singh ...'

'A Panjabi! A greengrocer, a widower and a Panjabi,' he shouted before she could finish.

As Mrs. Kumar settled in her favourite chair by the French windows she heard her husband slam shut his study door. He only reappeared for lunch and for afternoon tea. He was in his study when he heard Old 'enry Ford coming up the drive.

36

Deep didn't give Kavi a chance to switch off the engine and get out of the minivan. She was waiting on the front porch. She ran down the steps, wrenched open the passenger door, jumped in and slammed the door shut. Kavi, rather taken aback, asked if everything was alright. She nodded. 'Are you sure?' 'Yes!' she snapped. 'Please may we go.'

Her father saw everything through his study window. An old minivan! Bright green, orange and yellow! Making more noise than his drive-around lawnmower! The Apple Cart in large brown letters on the sides! And the greengrocer didn't even have the courtesy to open the door for the daughter of a merchant!

It was some while before Deep calmed down and realised how rude she had been. Kavi, for his part, couldn't get over how different she looked from the teacher he had seen at the parents' evening on Wednesday. She was beautiful. Her dark hair was so shiny. Her eyes – angry at he knew not what and framed by her dark eyebrows – were alight. Her pale-brown skin was smooth and unmarked.

She was wearing a dark green polo-neck sweater that went perfectly with the pale brown jacket and matching ankle-length skirt. 'I thought you wore glasses,' he said, keeping his eyes on the road and concentrating on his driving. Deep was impressed that he had remembered and explained they were for reading. 'And for marking test papers,' he said. She laughed and started to relax.

For the rest of the twenty minute journey she sat back and studied her escort. Kavi was wearing a dark brown suede leather jacket, beige-coloured casual trousers and dark brown suede shoes. His white silk shirt had a round collar that did not permit or need a tie. Deep noticed a hint of grey in his dark hair and neatly trimmed beard. She sensed in this man an inner confidence, a sureness of himself and of his abilities, together with an acceptance of his limitations. She also sensed a certain restlessness, an eagerness to know and learn from the people and the world around him. As Old 'enry Ford rattled to a halt outside Le Café Blanc Kavi said, 'I hope you like French cuisine.'

'Good evening Mr. Cheema,' said the Maître d'hôtel. 'We have not seen you for such a long time. Your table for two is ready. Please follow me.'

'Thank you, Henri.'

When they reached the candle-lit table in a nook by the stone fireplace, Henri pulled out a chair for Deep. 'S'il vous plaît, Mademoiselle!' he said, with a flourishing gesture that bade her sit down.

When they were both seated, Henri whisked the damask napkins from the table onto each of their laps then departed with another flourish: 'Bon appétit.'

'Good evening, Mr. Cheema,' said Claude, the wine waiter. 'Plum and grape juice for you, n'est-ce pas? Some wine perhaps for Mademoiselle?'

Kavi nodded then looked across the table at Deep who appeared even more stunning in the candle light.

'If it is non-alcoholic then I should like plum and grape juice, please,' said Deep.

'Bon! Chilled, oui?' said Claude who left before they could even nod their heads.

'I think,' said Kavi, 'that we should study the menu before the next assault. 'Would you like some help?'

Before she could say yes, the next wave arrived in the form of François. He introduced himself as their waiter for the evening and then rattled off the Chef's selection du soir.

'Merci, François,' said Kavi. 'We'd now like time to study the à la carte menu.'

'What do you recommend?' said Deep.

'French Onion soup – it has a melted gruyère crouton – as a starter followed by Poulet au Cidre Breton avec des petits pois et des pommes frites.'

'That sounds wonderful.'

'I suppose it does,' said Kavi. 'Chicken and chips with peas always sounds better in French.'

Deep laughed and Kavi noticed how white and even her teeth were.

'To finish, Mademoiselle, you must 'ave ze Crème Brûlée – ze spécialité de la maison, n'est-ce pas?' Just as Kavi said this in a mock heavy French accent, François returned.

'You are ready to order, n'est-ce pas?'

'Kavi and Deep looked at one another and burst out laughing.'

'So,' said Kavi, 'are you feeling alright now?'

'Yes, I am, thank you, Mr. Cheema.'

'Kavi! Please call me Kavi, Miss Kumar.'

'Only if you'll call me Deep.'

'Agreed but I thought your name was Deeptikana.'

'It is but I prefer Deep,' she said, wondering how he knew her full name.

'Well then, Deep, tell me how you knew about boys will be boys.'

'The Will Hay film you mean? Just one of those things. I like that kind of film. And before you even ask, Kavi, the answer is no – I do not like Bollywood movies.'

The soup was served. They both enjoyed every drop. Deep asked that they not talk shop, meaning she didn't want to talk about school. 'I understand,' said Kavi. 'You don't want to hear about the greengrocery business. You think fruit and vegetables boring.' When she tried to explain what she meant, Kavi held up his hand as she might have done to silence her class.

'Vegetables can be extremely interesting although not vegetables per se. Take these peas, for instance. How did they get out of their pods and end up here on my fork? Take these chips. Who peeled and cut up the potatoes? Might not the Le Café Blanc chef be exploiting young children labouring illegally in his kitchen?' Kavi immediately regretted his poor attempt at humour when he saw the look on Deep's face. 'I'm sorry,' he said, 'that was in bad taste. I've upset you. I hope I haven't spoilt your evening. Please forgive me.'

She shook her head. 'There's nothing to forgive,' she said, trying to put her father's business problem out of her mind. 'I nearly spoilt the evening before it started. It was my father, you see. It was so frustrating. He thought I needed his permission to dine with you. In some respects he is still living in the past. He went on about how Ghandi had to ask the Modh Bania permission to leave India...'

'...to study law at London University and be called to the bar at the Inner Temple,' interjected Kavi.

'Oh! Well, yes,' she said. 'I told him that we're British citizens and there's no caste system here.'

'Perhaps,' said Kavi, 'here in Britain it's called a class system.'

'Oh, I see what you mean. But there's no caste system like there is in India.'

'The Constitution of India of 1950 made the caste system illegal. So in theory there's no caste system in India. But as someone I know is fond of saying, the law is one thing – enforcement is another.'

François interrupted their conversation with 'Excusez-moi! Monsieur! Mademoiselle! Voilà – la crème brûlée. Bon appétit!'

'What exactly do you mean – the law is one thing – enforcement is another?'

'Let me ask you this,' said Kavi. 'What does this signify to you as a driver – a traffic sign with 50 in black letters on a white background inside a red circle?'

'A fifty mile per hour speed limit.'

'Correct. But what does it mean?'

'It means I should not drive faster than 50 miles per hour.'

'Correct. It is a limit. Unfortunately, the majority of drivers treat it as a target to be exceeded. They break the law and commit an offence. These offenders cause on average more than 100 deaths or injuries on the road each day.'

'Oh no,' whispered Deep under her breath as she remembered that Kavi's wife had been killed on the road.

'Oh yes,' said Kavi in an equally soft voice. 'The police (with the help of cameras) and the courts (by the application of fines, penalties and other punishments) try to enforce the law. Do you think they succeed?'

'No,' said Deep, 'I don't think they do.'

'Do you break the law?'

'No. At least I don't think so - not knowingly, anyway.'

'In the eyes of the law – not to be confused with justice - ignorance is no defence.' Then he paused, misunderstood the sad look on her face and said, 'I'm sorry, I'm riding my hobby-horse and starting to bore you.'

'Not at all,' said Deep. 'Please go on.'

François appeared once more to interrupt their conversation. 'Excusez-moi! Monsieur! Mademoiselle! Would you like to see the cheese board?' They shook their heads. 'Café?' Kavi ordered café noir. Deep order café au lait.

'Are you sure I'm not boring you?'

'No, Kavi, you're not, honestly.'

'Look, the law is a set of rules, often complicated rules, that we should all follow to live in peace and harmony with our neighbours in society. Justice is the exercise of authority in the maintenance of those rules. The task is to make everyone follow the rules and to punish those of us who don't.'

'But surely,' said Deep, 'the real task is to make us understand why we should follow the rules?'

'It sounds like you studied Dr John Dewey as well as Herr Friedrich Froebel when you were training to be a teacher.'

'How did you know I studied Froebel when I was at Maria Grey College?'

'Your qualifications on Beaconsfield staff register. NFF. National Froebel Foundation. Anyway, how did the story go now. Ah, yes, I remember.

A neighbour sees Dewey's son standing barefoot in a puddle.

The neighbour says, 'Shouldn't you make your son get out of that puddle, Dr Dewey?'

Dr Dewey replies, 'No, I should make him understand why he should get out.'

'What's wrong with that?' asked Deep.'

'Understanding why we should or should not do something does not mean that we will or will not do that something. In my experience, people do not always act according to their social conscience,' said Kavi somewhat angrily, thinking of the hit-and-run drunk driver who killed Marie Claire.

'How true,' said Deep somewhat sadly, thinking of her father's uncle in India.

As she drank her coffee, Deep thought how articulate and well informed Kavi was for – dare she share her father's prejudice - a greengrocer. Then she thought how expensive the meal would be and asked if they could share the bill. 'I appreciate your offer to go Dutch,' said Kavi, 'but this is my treat and not, as you agreed, a bribe.'

After Kavi had paid the bill, he asked the Maître d'hôtel if le Chef might spare a moment to have a word with him. A few minutes later le Chef arrived dressed in white and wearing his distinctive tall white hat. 'Jean-Paul,' said Kavi, shaking hands. 'Ça va?' Jean-Paul, grinning from ear to ear launched into a torrent of French.

At the earliest opportunity, Kavi introduced le Chef to Deep. Jean-Paul kissed the back of Deep's hand. and was into Enchanté, Mademoiselle. Je suis enchanté de faire votre connaisance, before Kavi interrupted. 'This is an evening of French cuisine but English conversation, mon ami.'

'Thank you so much. The food was delicious.' said Deep sincerely.

'But of course it was,' said Jean-Paul. 'That is why you come to Le Café Blanc, no?'

'Jean-Paul, please,' said Kavi. 'Of course the food is great. I dragged you out here because I want to know how the peas got out of their pods and onto my plate? How the potatoes got out of their skins and became the chips on my plate.'

'Peas? Non! Chips? Non! I, Jean-Paul, prepare only les petits pois et les pommes frites!'

'I know that, my friend,' said Kavi. 'What I don't know is who shells des petits pois and who peels the potatoes and cuts them into des pommes frites?'

'Ah. You think that I, Jean-Paul...'

'No, of course you don't shell peas and peel potatoes. But who does? Do you by any chance have children doing that?'

'Des enfants? Are you mad? Non. Pas du tout! I must go. A pleasure to meet you, Mademoiselle,' he said, kissing the back of her hand once more. 'Au revoir, mon vieux.'

Kavi said bonsoir to the Maître d'hôtel and led Deep by the arm to Old 'enry Ford.

It was just after 11 o'clock when Kavi brought the minivan as quietly as possible to a halt and walked Deep to her front door. The security porch light came on but her father's study remained in darkness. Her parents were already in bed. Her brother was watching television in his room at the back of the house. Kavi and Deep began to speak at the same time. They laughed. Kavi waited patiently.

'I have had a wonderful evening,' said Deep. 'Thank you so much for inviting me.' Kavi smiled, said what a pleasure it had been for him and hoped that they could do it again sometime in the not too distant future. 'I should like that very much,' said Deep, touching the sleeve of his jacket. Kavi smiled, kissed her on the forehead, said goodnight and walked down the steps to the minivan.

* * * * *

On the Monday, exactly one week after Bill Fosdyke had apprised him of Bhuvanesh and Prathamesh Kumar's possible involvement with child labour, Kavi and Raj took the train into town to spend the day in the South Kensington museums. Beaconsfield School was having a teachers training day. Raj tossed the coin. Kavi

44

called 'heads' and lost. So they went to the Science Museum in the morning – Raj's choice – and the Victoria & Albert in the afternoon – Kavi's choice. For the rest of the week it was school and The Apple Cart as usual.

On the same Monday, Deep did her best to concentrate on the teacher training but her mind kept drifting off, one minute to the evening out with Kavi and the next minute to her father's business problems, to child labour, the law and justice. She took note of what Mrs. Frobisher had to say on the subject of discipline in the classroom.

'As teachers,' said the femme formidable, 'we have a duty first to ensure that our pupils get into good habits. Respecting authority. Behaving themselves. Working hard. Doing their best. When they do the right thing as a matter of routine, then we have a duty to ensure that our pupils understand – as far as they can – the reasons for these good habits.'

This did not sound like the educational philosophy of Froebel or Dewey. Deep realised how much she would like to hear Kavi's comments on Mrs. Frobisher's views. For the rest of the week it was classes as usual.

On that same Monday, Amal was at his desk in the corner of the warehouse at 7 a.m. He was an hour earlier than usual and full of the joys of Spring in spite of the cold autumn weather. When Mukharjee arrived at a quarter to eight, he was surprised and somewhat disturbed to see Amal already at his desk. 'Ah, Mr Mukharjee, I see you have managed to drag yourself out of bed.' When Mukharjee said that he thought their meeting was for 8 o'clock, Amal said, 'Quite correct. 8 o'clock sharp. I am pleased to see you are early. You have passed the first test.' For the rest of the week Amal explained in detail to Mukharjee the business.

On that Monday when Kavi and Raj were travelling second class on the 9.15 train to Paddington, Mr. Prathamesh Kumar was travelling in a first class compartment two carriages away. His appointment with David Wong at Lincoln's Inn was for 10.15 a.m. He arrived some minutes early. At 10.14 a.m. Mandy took him to David's office, showed him to a seat and asked if he would like some coffee. He nodded. She left, saying that Mr. Wong would be along shortly. After what seemed ages but was in fact only two minutes, Mandy appeared with the usual tray of coffee, cream, sweeteners and chocolate biscuits.

At twenty past ten, David appeared. 'I'm sorry to have kept you waiting, Mr. Kumar. Ah, good. I see our Mandy has done her stuff. Now to business, so to speak. I'd like you to tell me about your relationship with Mr. Bhuvanesh Kumar.' When Prathamesh said simply that he was his uncle, David said, 'Yes. Yes, of course. What I meant was that I need to know everything about your business relationship with him.'

Prathamesh spent the rest of the week in his study either pouring over his books, contracts and other legal documents or talking on the telephone to his uncle in India.

* * * * *

'Do you need any fruit or vegetables, Mum?' I'm popping into The Broadway.' It was Saturday afternoon. Deep had finished her lesson preparations before lunch.

'Good! I am coming,' her mother said, 'Doctor Biswas said walking is good for heart.'

'You don't have to come. It's a bit windy this afternoon.'

'I am coming.'

They put on their warm coats, scarves, hats and gloves, waved goodbye to Prathamesh through his study window and set off arm-in-arm into the centre of what is known as Little India. Deep took the shortest route - past West Middlesex Golf Club where Mr. Kumar was a member – and within fifteen minutes of leaving their house they were window-shopping along the High Street and then The Broadway.

'That looks a good place for fruit and vegetables,' said Deep, pointing to The Apple Cart.'

46

'Yes, very good,' said her mother, suppressing a smile, and as they approached the stall, she let go of her daughter's arm.

'Good afternoon, Mrs. Kumar,' said Raj. 'How are you today?'

'I'm very well, Mr. Cheema. How are you?'

'I'm fine, thank you, Mrs. Kumar,' said Raj from behind the till.

Deep was speechless. She just stood staring at her mother until Raj said, 'Hello Miss. Come to buy some apples? They're fresh and juicy.'

Then Kavi appeared as if from nowhere and joined in. 'Mrs. Kumar. How nice to see you. Not too cold for you I hope.'

'No, not cold. It's nice to see you again. I believe you are knowing my daughter, Deep,' she said with a wry smile.

'I am privileged to say that I do know Raj's teacher,' Kavi said, looking at Deep and giving her his broadest smile. When he heard oh, oh, he turned towards his son and his smile vanished.

'I'm sorry, Dad. I forgot to give Miss Kumar your letter,' said Raj, reaching into his pocket. 'Sorry, Miss. It's a bit crumpled.'

Deep read the letter while Kavi and Raj served her mother with some guavas and papayas. Mrs. Kumar was impressed with how quickly Raj worked out in his head what she owed for the fruit and how confidently he handled the till, giving her the correct change from the ten pound note.

When she thanked him and addressed him as Mr. Cheema, Raj gave her his broadest smile. 'How like his grandfather,' she thought. 'He's going to be tall and handsome just like his father,' she said to herself, as she looked at Kavi and asked him in Hindi how his mother was.

Before he could answer, Ravinder Kumar heard a voice from the corner of the stall. 'Namastay, Smt. Kumar.' It was Mrs. Cheema. For the next fifteen minutes, the two ladies were engrossed in conversation and oblivious of anyone around them. During this

47

time Raj hid behind the till while Deep answered Kavi's letter by saying how much she would like to go into London on Sunday for a pub lunch. Kavi was delighted and arranged to collect her at 10 o'clock sharp.

* * * * *

'What? She is going to a pub with this greengrocer? Today? In London?'

'Please be calm,' said Ravinder Kumar to her husband. 'He is very good greengrocer. Eat some guava.'

'How can I be calm? A merchant's daughter is going to eat and drink with a greengrocer. And in a public place!'

'Eat your fruit,' said Ravinder, 'and do not be worrying.'

Pramathesh sat and ate some of the guava his wife had prepared. He started to calm down. The fruit was excellent. He ate the rest and asked his wife if there was more. She gave him some papaya – his favourite. When he'd finished eating he was, she thought, more calm than she had seen him in a while. 'Excellent fruit, Ravinder. Thank you.'

'Please, Pram, now go to your study and read your paper.'

He was in his study all relaxed and enjoying his newspaper when at 10 o'clock precisely he heard Old 'enry Ford rattle to a stop outside the front door. Before her father could get up from his chair and look out of his study window, Deep was in the passenger seat and Kavi was driving out of the gate. As Pramathesh was watching the minivan disappear out of the gate, his study door opened and Ravinder came in. 'I am bringing you some more papaya, Pram.'

Kavi parked the minivan at Southall station and a few minutes later they were boarding the train to Paddington. It was the shortest journey he'd ever known. He sat opposite Deep and couldn't take his eyes off her. Her face glowed with vitality. She was wearing a smart fur hat and gloves. Over her tailored trouser suit she was wearing a fleece-lined jacket. Her shoes were smart. They matched her gloves and hat. Nevertheless, they were a sensible flat-heeled pair of suede shoes suitable for long walks.

From Paddington he took her on the tube following the same route he had used the last time he came up to town to Lincoln's Inn. When they stepped out of the station into the bright sunshine, he directed her across High Holborn and into Chancery Lane. Kavi was wearing a warm overcoat over his polo-necked sweater, sports jacket and trousers. He too wore gloves and sensible shoes but he had no hat so the crisp autumn air ruffled his hair as they walked.

'I love this part of London,' said Deep. 'Chancery Lane. Inns of Court. So much history and tradition. Have you read Bleak House? Charles Dickens writes of dinosaur lawyers walking up and down this smog-filled street. And an old lawyer blows his brains out in a coffee-house in Chancery Lane.'

'Old Tom Jarndyce.'

'Yes that's the lawyer. Have you read the book or did you watch the television serial?'

'Both, actually but I preferred the book.' Then leading her through the Gatehouse, he said, 'Let's see if we can find Lincoln's Inn Hall where according to Dickens at the very heart of the fog,...'

'... sits the Lord High Chancellor in his High Court of Chancery,' said Deep.

According to a tablet on the north wall, the Old Hall was built in 1492 after Henry VII came to the throne. However, from 1924 to 1927 it was dismantled brick by brick, stone by stone to straighten the five-centuries old wooden rafters and preserve the building. Kavi pointed to the numbers on some of the bricks. 'All the bricks and stones were marked when they dismantled the Old Hall,' said Kavi, 'so it could be rebuilt exactly as it was first built five hundred years ago.' When Deep asked what the Old Hall is used for today, Kavi said, 'As a compulsory dining hall during the four legal terms (Hilary, Easter, Trinity and Michaelmas) and as the High Court of Chancery out of term time.'

'What do you mean – compulsory dining?'

'Before you can be called to the bar,' said Kavi, 'you must attend twelve qualifying sessions which involve dining in Hall. You have to be in your place when Grace is said at the start and at the end otherwise the session doesn't count. It's a tradition going back to the time when a young barrister learned the law from older barristers over a meal and a glass of wine.'

'So nowadays if you want to become a barrister, all you have to do is dine in the Old Hall twelve times,' she said with a wry look on her face.

Kavi laughed. 'I don't think it's that easy. Shall we go?'

'Where to now? Another Inn of Court?'

Leaving the grounds of Lincoln's Inn, they walked south to the end of Chancery Lane, crossed Fleet Street and entered Inner Temple Lane. At the end of the lane they came face to face with Temple Church. Deep loved this round building. Full of enthusiasm, she asked Kavi if he knew that this round church had been built by the Knights Templar in the 12th century and what did he think of the grotesque carvings at the top of the stone pillars supporting the Norman arches.

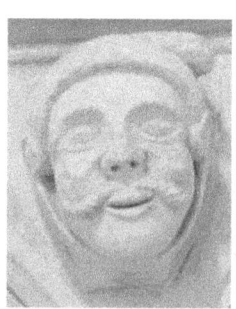  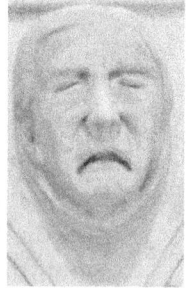

As soon as she'd asked, she thought how much she sounded like a teacher on a school trip. She was relieved when he said that he hadn't really noticed the carvings until she had pointed them out.

'The Inner Temple is where Ghandi was called to the bar,' said Kavi, as they walked down the steps and through the beautiful landscaped gardens towards Broad Walk and Victoria Embankment. 'Did I tell you that there are four Inns of Court to select, train and call lawyers to the bar? Gray's Inn, Lincoln's Inn, Middle Temple and Inner Temple, of course.' When Deep asked how he knew so much about the Inns of Court, barristers and the law, Kavi glanced at his watch and said, 'I don't know about you but I'm ready for lunch.'

'So much for your idea of a pub,' said Deep as they arrived at the George Inn – the last remaining galleried inn in London.

'It's a sort of old pub,' said Kavi. 'It was a 17th century coach terminus.'

'Dickens mentions it in his book Little Dorrit,' said Deep. 'I hope you don't want to sit outside.'

Kavi laughed. 'Not today.' And with that they went inside and sat in the corner on the bench just behind the door.

Over a lunch of cheese, home-made pickle, fresh home-baked bread, butter from a proper dish – not a little sealed plastic pot – and, to her delight, a glass of plum and grape juice, Deep told Kavi about Beaconsfield school's training day. They discussed Mrs. Frobisher's approach to classroom discipline. They talked about the films they had seen, the books they had read and the music they had listened to. The time flew by. Before they knew it they were on the tube to Paddington and on the train to Southall.

As Old 'enry Ford came to a halt outside her front door, Deep saw her father's face at his study window. When she asked Kavi if he would like to come in for a cup of tea, he smiled and said, 'Another time perhaps. Mother will be waiting to serve supper. I really enjoyed your company today. I hope you enjoyed our trip.' She answered by leaning over and kissing him on the cheek. Then she was out of the van and hurrying indoors.

* * * * *

At the end of school on Monday, the day after her trip to London, Miss Kumar gave Raj a sealed envelope with strict instructions to deliver it to his father or suffer the consequences. On that same Monday, Deep's father caught the early train to London to spend another day with his lawyers at Lincoln's Inn. Amal left the house early, actually before anyone else was awake. He was eager to be at The Apple Cart before six o'clock – the time when Mr. Cheema said he would start teaching him the business. Mrs. Kumar left the empty house to join Mrs. Cheema for morning coffee at Oswald Road.

Kavi smiled when he saw Amal reading the detailed restrictions on the loading/unloading traffic sign near the stall. 'Good morning, Mr. Kumar. I'm glad to see you're here bright and early.'

'What time do they deliver your fruit and vegetables?'

'Oh,' said Kavi, 'everything is always unloaded and into the stall before 6 o'clock.'

'Is there ever any problem with deliveries? Our carpets didn't always arrive on time.'

'Ah, well,' said Kavi, 'you can't always rely on other people to do the right thing.'

'So how do we make sure your fruit and vegetables are here before 6 o'clock?'

'Good question. I'll let you in on our trade secret later. First, let's open up the stall and I'll show you how the morning normally begins.' And of course it began with Amal putting the wooden cart outside, polishing the apples one by one and carefully assembling them into a pyramid.

At about 11 o'clock, Kavi glanced at his watch. 'Time for another coffee break. You can close up and we'll pop back to Oswald Road. We shall need the van for our next task.' Amal's eyes lit up at the prospect of driving Old 'enry Ford again.

As they stepped through the front door into the hallway they heard voices coming from the living room. It was definitely not Mrs.

Cheema's radio broadcasting in Panjabi. They hung up their outdoor coats and Kavi led the way into the living room.

'Good morning, ladies,' said Kavi. 'How are you both today?'

Amal was speechless when he saw his mother.

'Good morning, Amal,' chimed the two women. Then his mother said, 'Do not be being surprised, Amal. Mrs. Kumar is telling me about new job and all that. When will you be telling your father?'

Amal followed Kavi into the kitchen where they sat on stools and drank their coffee. 'So, that lady is your mother,' said Kavi, 'and your father imports carpets from India?'

'Yes,' said Amal.

'Do you by any chance have a sister?'

'Yes,' said Amal. 'She's a teacher. She's at Beaconsfield School.

When they had finished their coffee, Kavi gave Amal the van keys. When he asked where they were going, Kavi said, 'your place to pick up your stuff. Starting today, you live here, remember?' Amal's mother refused their offer of a lift. She and Mrs. Cheema still had a lot to talk about and Dr. Biswas had told her walking was good for her heart.

When they returned to Oswald Road with the few things that Amal felt he needed, his mother had already left. Mrs. Cheema showed him his room. When they had emptied the van, they walked back to the stall in The Broadway. Later that afternoon Raj arrived at The Apple Cart and gave his dad the envelope from his teacher.

While Kavi read Deep's note, Raj showed Amal how to handle the till. When Amal asked about the float and how they handled the petty cash, he was impressed by how much Raj knew about the business. He hadn't known as much about the carpet business when he was eleven. 'Time to shut up the stall and go home,' said Kavi. 'We've an early start tomorrow.' Over the evening meal Amal learned the trade secret of the fruit and vegetable deliveries. 'Yes,' said Kavi, 'We'll get up at 3 o'clock and be at New Covent Garden Market by 4 a.m. Oh, and by the way, my name is Kavi – not Kevin or Kev – understood.'

Over the next four weeks, Amal and Raj proved their reliability, Amal as manager of the business and Raj as courier of sealed envelopes between his teacher and his father. Mrs. Cheema was glad of Amal's company especially when her grandson accompanied Kavi and Deep on their Sunday trips to London. Sometimes she would help Amal at the stall. Raj helped at the till all day Saturday and for an hour after school during the week.

Kavi was gradually able to give more time and thought to the legalities of child labour in India. After the first two weeks, Kavi left Amal to cope on his own – The Apple Cart was now open six days a week – and went up to Lincoln's Inn for an 11 o'clock Monday morning appointment. It was Kavi's first one since his father had passed away.

* * * * *

'Mr. Cheema will see you now,' said Mandy.

'Please sit down,' said Kavi. 'May we offer you some coffee.' When his client shook his head, Mandy gathered up the tray from the desk and wiggled out of the room.

When the door had closed, Kavi looked up from the bulky file open in front of him and said, 'Your uncle may, I fear, be in serious trouble, Mr. Kumar, and in my professional opinion there is very little we can do to help him. The laws of England and India have much in common, of course, but it's really a matter of jurisdiction.'

'So,' said Pramathesh, 'there is nothing you can do for him?'

'No, I'm afraid not. I assume that he has consulted lawyers in Uttar Pradesh?

'Uncle Bhuvanesh thinks all lawyers are crooks – leeches to suck his blood – if you'll pardon me for saying so.'

'That's not uncommon amongst people who do not understand the complexities and subtleties of the law,' said Kavi, 'let alone appreciate the qualifications, training, experience and effort required of lawyers to interpret the law and plead a client's case. You are, I understand, a professional man yourself, Mr. Kumar. Do you share your uncle's view of lawyers?'

'No, I do not but I admit that we may always find a few rotten apples in a barrel be it one of lawyers or one of accountants.'

The two men smiled at one another in agreement then Kavi said, 'As regards your own position in this matter, I should like to clarify one or two points.' Turning over a page in the file on his desk, he asked, 'What was your official position in East India Woollen & Silk Carpets Ltd when your father died and you took over the company?'

'My father was the principal shareholder, chairman of the board and general manager of our private, family company. I was company treasurer. When my father died I inherited his shares and became the chairman.'

'Did Mr. Bhuvanesh Kumar ever hold shares in your company?'

'No. Never,' he said emphatically. 'Ours is a British business with no base in India.'

'Did your company ever employ Mr. Bhuvanesh Kumar in any capacity?

'No. Never. He has always worked quite independently of us.'

'Is Mr. Bhuvanesh Kumar a sole proprietor or a sole trader?

'He is a sole proprietor. He owns and runs a shop where his carpets are made. I suppose he could also be a sole trader because, to my knowledge, he only deals with carpets.'

'Mr. Bhuvanesh Kumar has never been under contract to your father or your company to make carpets just for your father or your company?'

'No.'

'So your father or your company could not instruct him to use child labour? And neither your father nor your company ever did issue any such instructions?' When the man sitting opposite him hesitated, Kavi said, 'Let me put this another way, Mr. Kumar. If your father had told your uncle to use child labour, would your uncle have had to do what your father told him? May I remind you that your father was senior to Mr. Bhuvanesh Kumar. He was head of the Kumar family and, by tradition, to be respected and obeyed.'

Pramathesh Kumar was beginning to feel uncomfortable. This tall, soft-spoken lawyer seemed to be cross-questioning him as though he were in the witness box and on trial. He knew his father had told his uncle to make the dhurries and the hand-knotted carpets as quickly and cheaply as possible. On the one hand, he could never believe his father would have told uncle Bhuvanesh to use children. On the other hand, he knew in his heart that children cost less than adults, that their fingers are nimble and that they need less light to work by. What he didn't know – or perhaps didn't want to know – was that these children usually became severely ill by the time they were adults, suffering eye damage from the poor light and lung diseases from the dust and carpet fluff.

'My father was an honourable man. He would never have done such a thing.'

'Did your father ever visit his brother in Bhadohi?'

'He saw my uncle when they attended my grandfather's funeral.'

'Have you ever visited your uncle?'

'No. I never seemed to have had the time.'

'Does your uncle have a large family?'

'He has three sons and two daughters.'

'Does he have any grandchildren?'

56

'I think so. I'm not sure. Why are you asking me these family questions?

'Many employers of child labour use a loophole that puts family members outside the protection of the law. In addition to using their own sons and daughters, grandsons and granddaughters, cousins, nephews and nieces, these employers often claim as family the young children they buy – and even steal – from parents and guardians.'

Pramathesh looked aghast. 'That's criminal.'

'Indeed it is,' said Kavi. 'So you see, I need to know more about your uncle's operation and, more importantly, how much you and your father may have known.'

Pramathesh looked at his watch. 'Do you have any more questions? I'm feeling unwell.'

'Just one more for now,' said Kavi. 'Do your imported carpets carry the RUGMARK trademark?'

'I'm sorry,' said Pramathesh, 'I don't know what that is. I've never heard of it.'

'RUGMARK. A voluntary program launched in 1994 to certify Indian carpets made without the use of child labour. I suggest you look into it,' said Kavi, getting to his feet.

'Thank you. I shall.'

'Whatever your uncle has been up to, you and your company may have nothing to worry about legally at the moment,' said Kavi, opening the door, 'but we're not out of the woods yet. I bid you good day.' As Pramathesh walked away down the corridor Kavi said softly under his breath, 'If you've any heart at all, Mr. Kumar, you should have plenty on your conscience.'

* * * * *

It took four weeks for Pramathesh, Amal and Kavi to make up their minds and decide what to do. All three men decided to take action on the very same day – on the Sunday – after they had talked things over with their confidantes.

For the first time in a very long time Pram sat across from his wife in her sewing room. Even at this time in the year there was some colour in their garden. No, not their garden – Ravinder's garden. The deciduous trees were preparing for winter by losing their leaves. The evergreen shrubs – the laurels and holly – would hold onto their tough waxy ones and display their berries in spite of any frost and snow. Pram began to see why his wife loved to sit in her room and look through the French window at such a restful, tranquil scene.

'What are you wanting to tell me, Pram?'

'It's about the company, Ravinder. I want to sell it and retire.'

'I am thinking that this is good thing to do. I am very happy to hear this.'

'I also want to take you on a voyage of discovery to India.'

'That would be very nice, Pram. Thank you. Will you be telling Amal?'

'Yes, of course, and Deep.'

Ravinder smiled to hear him call their daughter Deep instead of Deeptikana – his beam of light. 'Please be telling them this morning. Amal is coming soon to collect more things from his room. Deep is going out again.

58

'With the greengrocer, I suppose,' sighed Pram. 'I am going to my study to read the paper. Let me know when he arrives.'

'I think you will be hearing him,' she said with a smile. 'Would you like some guava?'

In spite of encouragement from Mrs. Cheema, Amal was still rather nervous as he approached the front door of his parents' house and parked Old 'enry Ford on the drive in sight of his father's study. He hadn't lied to his father. He was the business manager. He did manage the stall. And he was enjoying every minute – even, to his own surprise, getting up at 3 o'clock in the morning. The pay wasn't great but, as he'd come to realise, money isn't everything. When he got out of the van and walked up the steps towards the front door, he caught sight of his father looking out of the study window. He waved. To his astonishment, his father waved back.

'Hello Dad!'

'Amalesh! What are you doing with that van?'

'I'm using it to collect some of my stuff,' said Amal with a smile.

'That's the greengrocer's van, isn't it?

'Yes Dad.'

'So why are you driving it?'

'Because I'm the greengrocer now.'

Pramathesh fell back into his big leather chair and listened while Amal told him how he got the job, how hard he was working and how much he was enjoying the work.

'Amal,' said Pramathesh, using the name his son preferred and always wanted his father to use, 'I am selling the company. I am going to retire and take your mother on holiday to India.'

'Good for you, Dad. You both deserve it. Mum's always wanted to visit India.'

'Would you like to come with us?'

'I'd like to Dad but I am too busy right now. Thanks all the same.'

'Would you like me to help you with your stuff?'

'Thanks, Dad. Cool!' And it was especially cool when his mum helped as well.

When Old 'enry Ford had disappeared noisily out of the gate, Pram and Ravinder sat in her sewing room to enjoy the peace and quiet.

Deep wanted to clean and tidy her room before washing her hair and getting ready to see Kavi. Over the noise of the vacuum, she hadn't heard Amal's voice but at one point she happened to look out of her bedroom window. There was The Apple Cart minivan parked in front of the house. She panicked as she imagined the confrontation of merchant v. greengrocer.

Deep dropped the vacuum and dived into the shower. She dried her hair as quickly as possible and was just putting on some casual clothes when she heard the noise of the minivan. When she looked out of her bedroom window she saw Old 'enry Ford's rear end disappearing through the gateway at the bottom of the drive.

'Hello, Deep,' said her father, as she dashed into her mother's sewing room.

'Was that The Apple Cart minivan I saw leaving here a minute ago?'

'Yes,' said her mother, 'but it wasn't your greengrocer friend driving. It was Amal.'

'Amal! Amal was driving it?'

'Yes, Deep,' said her mother. 'Did you know he's the manager of the stall now?'

'Amal's the manager of The Apple Cart? Would you believe it! What do you think of that, Dad?' she said, forgetting herself. Before he could answer, the three of them heard the front door bell. Deep dashed back upstairs to tidy her hair. From her bedroom window she saw a car parked on the drive.

She was surprised. Nobody had heard it arrive. Amal could have told her it was a BMW 5 series saloon.

Her father who saw it from his study window could have told her it cost a lot of money. Mrs. Kumar put down her sewing and went to answer the door. When she saw who was standing in the porch, she smiled and said, 'Please come in.' Then she knocked on her husband's study door, opened it and said, 'There's a gentleman to see you, Pram.' Ravinder smiled to herself as she retreated and closed the study door behind her.

'Good morning, Mr. Kumar,' said Kavi. 'I have come to plead the case for a greengrocer who wishes to become engaged to your daughter.'

* * * * *

Epilogue

The characters, the East India Woollen & Silk Carpets Ltd and the events in my story are fictional but the poverty and the exploitation of children in India are matters of fact.

India has more than 1 billion people. 250 million are below the poverty line and three-quarters of the poor are in rural areas. More than 40% of the population over the age of 15 are illiterate. Of the 33 million or so children under 14 years of age at least 300,000 are estimated to work in Uttar Pradesh mostly in its hand-woven carpet industry spread over 2000 sq. kms. The Indian government estimates the number of child workers in all industries to be 12 million but other NGOs (non-government organisations) estimate numbers as high as 20 million. Child labour in India is deemed necessary for poor families to earn an income.

On the 25th July 1995, Congressman Dan Burton, testified before Congress on The Exploitation of Child Labour in India. He reported that child labour is a main component of the carpet industry, that many children are separated from their families to work 12 hours a day with only short breaks for meals of minimal staple and that the law (against employing children under age 14) is rarely followed and does not apply to the employment of family members. Congressman Burton also testified that employers often circumvent the law by claims of hiring distant family and that in rural areas there are few enforcement mechanisms and the punishments for violation are minimal or non-existent.

The Anti-Slavery Society, formed in 1983, is a public charity and one of many such organisations seeking to relieve the suffering of child bonded labourers. It promotes 'Rugmark' hand-woven carpets which carry a guarantee against the use of child labour. World Vision International is 'a Christian relief, development and advocacy organisation dedicated to working with children, families and communities to overcome poverty and injustice.' It promotes sponsorship for the education and welfare of children.

SEARIC is the registered charitable Society for the Education and Assistance of Rural Indian Children established in 2006 in Edmonton, Alberta by a small group of individuals initially to provide financial support for a rural school in Andhra Pradesh. In the early years of its formation I served as Secretary. My wife and I are now life members.

* * * * *

ACROSS A CROWDED ROOM

On the 6th of August 2010, on the cruise liner Celebrity Constellation, Maureen and I celebrated our Golden Wedding Anniversary. This is the story of how I met my wife. Some of my scientific friends suggest we travel through life encountering people haphazardly as particles collide according to Einstein's mathematical theory of random walk. Maureen and I met by chance they say. Some of my non-scientific friends suggest otherwise. It was kismet they say. Whatever the case, of one thing I can be absolutely sure, I am glad we met.

* * * * *

Maureen and I went to the same school. Well it was almost the same one. I went to Merrywood Grammar School for Boys. Maureen went to Merrywood Grammar School for Girls. The two school buildings were mirror images of each other, linked at the front by an archway leading to an open courtyard. The design of the two buildings and the vigilance of the teaching staff kept most of the boys and girls apart most of the time. This, and the fact that I entered and left the school three years before Maureen, certainly kept us apart. I never met Maureen at school.

In 1952 I went up to the University of Bristol Faculty of Science to read Chemistry. Three years later Maureen went up to the University of Bristol Faculty of Arts to read French. When I graduated in 1955 I still had not met Maureen. So what quirk of fate brought us together?

* * * * *

From my first day at university, or perhaps even before I went up, I resolved to work hard and play hard. The lectures and laboratory practicals guaranteed the hard work. It was up to me to choose the hard play. I played basketball and eventually became secretary of the men only basketball club. I attended the student chemical society lectures and eventually became secretary of the Student Chemical Society (otherwise known as the Chem. Soc.). You could be forgiven for thinking that neither activity would bring Maureen and me together. I should be inclined to agree with you if I did not know otherwise.

I know the basic steps of the waltz and at one time I managed the basic steps of the quickstep but I have never been good at dancing or particularly fond of that activity. Nevertheless, I resolved to attend one formal Ball each year. I did. They were grand black bow tie affairs. On each of the first two occasions I escorted a young lady from Merrywood Grammar School for Girls. She was not Maureen.

My first year of research for my PhD was spent in Holland. In my second year of research back in Bristol I became engaged. It was not to Maureen. And the engagement was not to last. When I began my third year of research, now disengaged, I was fully occupied

66

with my experiments and my duties as Student Chem. Soc. Secretary.

In my first undergraduate year, I dutifully attended not only the Chem. Soc. Lectures but also the Chem. Soc. Christmas Party. It was a shameful affair. It was held in a pub. Almost none of the female undergraduates came. Those that did were, I believe, suitably revolted at the sight of lecturers, including some senior lecturers, rapidly becoming drunk and bringing up their boots. I left early. I believe the like-minded students did too.

The second and last Chem. Soc. Christmas Party I attended was five years later when, as Secretary, I felt duty bound not only to attend but also to persuade the committee not to hold it in a pub. Foolishly overestimating my influence on the Chem. Soc. President, I called a meeting of all undergraduate and postgraduate chemistry students.

It was well attended especially by the female students many of whom were, I fear, persuaded by my vow to prevent the Christmas Party from becoming a drunken affair held in a pub. To my utter shame and dismay I failed. The party was held in a pub. It was a drunken affair. My sober friends and I left very early that Saturday. On the Monday I called another meeting.

* * * * *

At this second meeting which was well attended mainly by the students, male and female, who shared my disgust at the previous Saturday night's fiasco, I apologised for letting everybody down and invited all present to come to my Christmas Party at which there would be dancing and games, food and drink but NO alcohol. I was overwhelmed not only by the numbers wanting to come but also by their insistence on sharing the cost of hiring the hall and providing the food and drink. An undergraduate in his third year and working in my laboratory on his honours project was especially helpful.

Jack persuaded me to drive him into the countryside one evening after dark so he could cut holly from a hedgerow and shin up some trees and pick bunches of mistletoe. I thought Jack was slightly potty but I had to admit that the holly and mistletoe added

67

significantly to the Christmas decorations which he helped me to hang around the hall. Jack offered to help me in another way.

'Would you like me to ask my girl friend to bring a girl friend along for you?'

'There's no need,' I may have said, thinking that I would be too busy acting as MC.

'I know she has a friend who would like to come,' said Jack.

Our party took place on the Saturday following the disastrous Chem. Soc. Booze up. We held it in the Co-operative Society Hall not far from where I lived with my parents and six other students. The hall was rectangular, quite big and much longer than it was wide. At one end was a raised platform upon which I, the master of ceremonies stood almost the whole evening. At the other end, and to the side, was a single door – the entrance and exit.

As the revellers arrived, mostly in pairs, they were invited to collect a sheet and move around the room to play the first game - name the products from the advertisements pinned on the wall. We had of course cut the words out of the adverts. Jack was one of the last to arrive. He was accompanied by two female students. One had dark hair. The other had fair hair.

* * * * *

In 1947 James A. Michener won the Pulitzer Prize for his book Tales of the South Pacific. In 1949 Richard Rodgers composed the music and Oscar Hammerstein wrote the lyrics for one of the greatest Broadway musicals – South Pacific. In 1950 the musical won the Pulitzer Prize for Drama. Songs such as Bali Ha'i, I'm Gonna Wash That Man Right Outta My Hair, Younger than Springtime and I'm in Love with a Wonderful Guy became smash hits. My favourite was, and still is, Some Enchanted Evening.

That Saturday became my enchanted evening when I saw the stranger across that crowded room. I certainly knew I should see her again and again. I had found my true love and I felt her call me across that crowded room. So I flew to her side to make her my own because I did not wish all through my life to dream alone. Actually, what I did was to abandon my post on the raised platform to speak to Jack.

He introduced me to the student with the fair hair. Her name was Annette. It was his girl friend's friend! Maureen was Jack's girl friend! I returned to the platform and might have stayed there for the rest of the evening if Maureen had not asked me to dance. The party was a great success. Afterwards Jack, Maureen, Annette and a few close friends came back to my house to chat and play a few more games. I walked Annette home – she lived quite nearby – and apologised for having spent little time with her that evening.

* * * * *

The Christmas holiday came and went. On Wednesday the 1st January 1958 the European Economic Community Treaty came into force. I never noticed. On Saturday the 4th January, after ninety-two days in orbit, the Russian satellite, Sputnik 1, returned to earth; it actually fell to earth. I never noticed. On Monday the 6th January, I returned to the lab. When Jack arrived, I wished him a happy new year and asked how his girl friend was.

'She's not my girl friend anymore,' he said. 'We've split up.'

'Oh, too bad,' I said trying to sound sympathetic but failing utterly because in the next breath I said, 'What's Maureen's telephone number?'

Once I had found her, I never let her go.

* * * * *

Epilogue

The Co-operative Society Hall could be hired for a modest sum but no alcohol was permitted on the premised. The party was a success and nobody felt the need to drink in order to be merry. Needless to say, it was the most significant event in my life. I can still see in my mind's eye Maureen entering the hall and feel my heart beating faster. I forever thank my lucky stars for my wife, my closest companion and my dearest friend for more than fifty-four years.

* * * * *

THE DISAPPEARING CHEMISTRY TEACHER

The central incident in this story occurred in 1960 during my first year of full-time teaching and is described as accurately as my memory will allow. I have given fictitious names to the school and the people involved just in case the long arm of the law could stretch 50 years back in time and instigate prosecutions under the 1974 Health and Safety at Work Act.

* * * * *

News, especially bad news, travels fast anywhere. In the school where I began my career as a chemistry teacher in Britain, the rumour of Dr Harold Dainton's mishap travelled so fast that my colleagues in the Physics Department questioned Einstein's theory that nothing can travel faster than the speed of light. I had assembled most of the pieces of the story several days before I was able to speak to Harry himself.

The Laboratory at Bishop Moncton

The teaching laboratory I shared with Harry was on the far side of the school at the end of the main science corridor. The only door in and out was directly opposite the steps down to the basement corridor that led to the prep room and the laboratory technician's hideout.

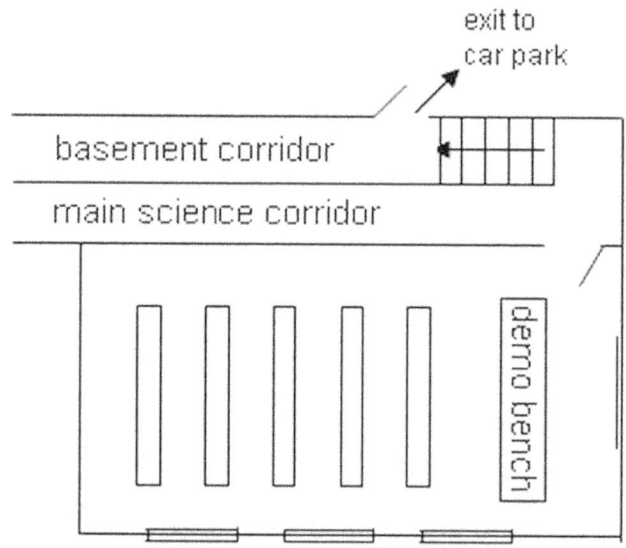

On the right, at the bottom of the steps, was the fire exit to the school car park. There were five laboratory benches for the pupils who faced the teacher's demonstration bench and the blackboard on the wall behind it. The blackout curtains were usually drawn across the three windows on the pupils' right (the teacher's left) to keep out the sun. Harry and I invariably kept the laboratory door open during our lessons. The Friday afternoon in question was no exception.

The Laboratory Technician

It was Friday afternoon and school had finished for the day. I put my nose round the door of the laboratory where our technician was clearing the mess on the demonstration bench. 'Sorry to trouble you, Bert,' I said. 'Have you seen Dr. Dainton?'

'He's gone I think, Sir.'

'Really? That's a nuisance. I wanted a word.'

'Well, I think he's gone, Sir. I'm pretty sure it was him dashing out the fire exit a few minutes before the bell. In a devil of a hurry he was.'

'The demo bench looks a bit of a mess, Bert.'

'No worse than usual, Sir, on a Friday afternoon when Dr Dainton's been enjoying himself. When he first started here, about thirty years ago, he...'

'Sorry, Bert. Can't stop. See you tomorrow morning.'

The Head of Chemistry

Dr Jacob Fothergill was Head of Chemistry and a man with strong views on what to teach and how to teach it. He was particularly keen on exciting demonstrations to capture the boys' interest and frequently referred to *Lecture Experiments in Chemistry* by George Fowles. The copy on his desk was signed by Fowles himself.

Dr Fothergill had started his meteoric career under George Fowles at Latymer Upper. On my first day at the school Dr Fothergill introduced me to the man I could turn to for help with demonstrations – Dr Harry Dainton. This introduction, as I later discovered, served at least two purposes. First, it placed me under the supervision of someone other than Dr Fothergill himself. Second, it re-ignited Harry's enthusiasm and innovative spirit.

Before my first class on Saturday morning I encountered Dr Fothergill in the corridor outside his office.

'Ah, Michael. Glad I caught you. Have you seen Harry?'

'No, sorry. As a matter of fact I was about to ask you that.'

'Bert seems to think he dashed off early yesterday afternoon. Before the bell! Very odd! That's not like Harry. He usually hangs around after school trying out some new experiment or other. Which reminds me,' said Dr Fothergill, 'What did you think of those competition reactions he showed us yesterday lunchtime?'

'Excellent. I'm going to demonstrate them to my Upper Fourths on Tuesday,' I answered.

'Make sure you give Bert a chitty today. He'll want plenty of notice to get the chemicals ready for you.'

'I've already seen Bert. Yesterday afternoon as a matter of fact.'

'Good man. Bert's pretty efficient but I suggest you weigh out the quantities yourself just to be on the safe side.'

'I've already told Bert to weigh out the metal powders and oxides on separate pieces of paper so I can check the weights and make up the mixtures in front of the class. I'm going to get one or two of the boys to assist.'

'Good idea.'

'By the way,' I said, 'I liked Harry's idea of using lead oxide with zinc, aluminium and magnesium as the first three mixtures and then using copper oxide with zinc, aluminium and magnesium in that order for the last three. The zinc with lead oxide was pretty tame but that magnesium copper oxide was something else.'

'It certainly was,' said Dr Fothergill. 'I noticed Harry only used a small amount of the mixture but I felt the heat on my face when it went off. I'm glad I was standing well back'

'I believe Harry did those demonstrations in the last double period yesterday afternoon. I wanted to ask him how they went.'

'There's the bell,' said Dr Fothergill. 'See you in the staff common room at break.'

The Chemistry Class

Saturday morning school came and went. There was no sign of Harry who, incidentally, was a bachelor living with his mother. On Saturday afternoons he often came to watch one of the school rugby matches even though, in deference to his years, he was no longer required to coach a team or referee a match. Nobody saw him that Saturday. He was not at the morning or evening service in the school chapel on Sunday. On Monday there was still no sign of him when the bell rang for the start of the first period. As it happened I shared a class with Harry as well as a laboratory.

'Good morning, Sir.'

'Good morning, boys,' I said to the class that Harry had seen for the final double period of school on the Friday afternoon.

'Be seated.' They sat down rather noisily.

'Less noise if you please, Gentlemen,' I said, as I started to hand back their notebooks.

'Sir!'

'Yes! What is it, Smithson?'

'Have you seen Dr Dainton, Sir?'

'Why do you ask?'

'Well, Sir, it's about his lesson last Friday.'

'What about it?'

'Well, Sir, you see, he sort of vanished in a cloud of smoke.'

'What do you mean, vanished?'

'Well, Sir, he was showing us some composition reactions...'

'Competition reactions, Sir,' piped up Hadrill, the boffin in the class whose father was the Director of the Ministry of Defence Chemical Research Establishment at Porton Down. 'He was demonstrating how a metal can displace a less reactive metal from its oxide.'

'That's what I said, Hadders,' retorted Smithson.

'No you didn't,' said Hadrill. 'You said composition not competition, you twerp.'

'Thank you, Gentlemen. I can do without this bickering. Perhaps you would be kind enough to tell me what happened, Hadrill.'

'Certainly, Sir. Well, Sir, Dr Dainton put six different mixtures of a metal powder and an oxide on fireproof asbestos mats on the demonstration bench,' said Hadrill looking at a table in his rough notebook.'

metal powder	metal oxide	observations	conclusion
zinc	lead oxide	flame – powder turned yellow then white later	Zn > Pb
aluminium	lead oxide	flame – mixture glowed hot	Al > Pb
magnesium	lead oxide	mixture flashed – heat given out	Mg > Pb
zinc	copper oxide	green flame – fluffy white powder formed	Zn > Cu
aluminium	copper oxide	mixture flashed – green flame – lots of heat	Al > Cu
magnesium	copper oxide		

I walked over to where Hadrill was sitting and looked at his book.

76

'Neat work, Hadrill, but where are your observations for the magnesium powder and copper oxide mixture? Didn't Dr Dainton do that demonstration?'

'Oh, yes, he did that one, Sir. It was the last one he did.'

'It was the last one he did alright, Sir,' piped up Smithson.

'Oh shut up!' said Hadrill. 'Sir, Dr Dainton did do all six reactions. I drew a diagram of the demonstration bench.'

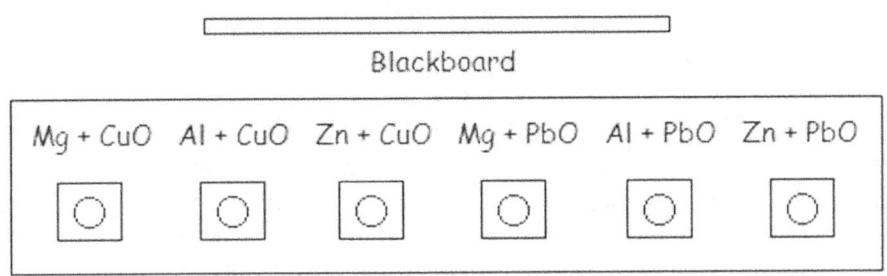

I looked at his diagram and asked the class, 'Why did Dr Dainton spread the mixtures out along the bench? Yes, Smithson!'

'For safety reasons, Sir.'

'Yes, Hadrill.'

'He didn't want one reaction to set off the one next to it, Sir. He didn't want to start a chain reaction.'

'Very good. Did Dr Dainton demonstrate the reactions in order from right to left as you look at the bench?'

'Yes, Sir,' said Hadrill. 'He did the Zn and PbO first and the Mg and CuO last. The reactions went much as we predicted. Copper oxide was more reactive than lead oxide. Magnesium was more reactive than zinc.'

'Sir,' chimed in Smithson, 'The last one – the magnesium and copper oxide – was brilliant. I felt the heat from back here on the third bench.'

'Please, Sir,' said Beechwood, a timid, bespectacled little fellow, 'Smithson's right, Sir. That last reaction was fantastic. And, Sir, Dr Dainton disappeared, Sir.'

'What do you mean by disappeared, Beechwood?'

'Well, Sir. When he lit the last mixture, there was a terrific flash and a huge cloud of smoke, Sir. When the smoke cleared, Dr Dainton had disappeared, Sir. He'd vanished!'

'That's right, Sir,' said Smithson. 'We haven't seen him since.'

The Chemistry Master

When Dr Harold Dainton turned up at school on the Tuesday morning he was looking exceedingly the worse for wear. From a distance he looked like a boiled lobster wearing white goggles over his eyes and a bandage over his large right claw. Close up I could see that his normally pale face was burned as though he had been out in a dry desert for a week under a fierce noonday sun. His sandy-coloured eyebrows had gone. His hairless, red face was in sharp contrast to the top of his head. His scalp was its normal pale colour and still sparsely covered by a layer of wispy, sandy-coloured hair. 'Harry! Where have you been? What have you been up to?'

'All my fault, old boy. I should have known better.'

'I gather it was your competition reactions. I had our Upper Fourths yesterday. According to Beechwood, you vanished in a cloud of smoke.'

'I suppose that's what it would have looked like to them.'

'So what happened?'

'My fault. You remember those reactions I showed you and Jacob at lunchtime last Friday. Well I thought they'd be a bit more exciting if I doubled the quantities. The first five reactions worked a treat. Great fun! The last one was the problem.

It wouldn't start. So I held a burning wax taper to the mixture. It went off like a bomb. I felt the heat on my face. I knew I was in trouble, so I dashed straight out the door, down the stairs to the basement exit, jumped in the car and drove straight to the hospital. The boys couldn't have seen me for smoke dust, you might say.'

'How come your eyelids and the skin around your eyes aren't burnt?' I asked.

'Saved by my Woolworth spectacles,' he said, handing them to me. The glass in the frames was scarred, deeply pitted and even melted in places.

'Crikey, you were lucky, Harry,' I said. 'Without these you would probably have lost your other eye.'

'Quite likely, old boy,' he said with a laugh. 'Anyway, the boys won't easily forget those demonstrations, will they.'

* * * * *

Epilogue

On the 31st July 1974, the Health and Safety at Work Act came into force. Its aim was to (a) secure the health, safety and welfare of persons at work, (b) protect others against risks to health or safety in connection with the activities of persons at work, (c) control the keeping and use and to prevent the unlawful acquisition, possession and use of dangerous substances, and (d) control certain emissions into the atmosphere.

Schools, colleges and universities came under the act, being regarded as places of work even if, in the opinion of some teachers and professors, the inactivity of pupils and students sometimes indicated otherwise. As a result, the one-eyed Dr Dainton and his like have become relics of a by-gone age. Many of the demonstrations that excited me as a pupil and that I performed as a chemistry teacher have been banned or confined to video clips to be watched on a computer screen.

I have a confession to make. Throughout my entire teaching career I continued to demonstrate many hazardous and exciting chemical reactions but I always took every possible safety measure. And I always made sure that my pupils understood the precautions I was taking and the hazards we were facing. More than seven thousand people, many of them school children, died in traffic incidents annually in the 1950s but no teacher or a pupil, to my knowledge, was ever killed by a chemical demonstration.

* * * * *

AN ALARMING BUSINESS

This story is set in Broadstone, Dorset, where I lived and worked from the Easter of 1971 until I moved to Canada in December 2000. The characters and their goings-on are figments of my imagination but inspired by certain events in which I was involved and by some people whom I held in high regard and about whom I should not, nay would not intentionally write a libellous word.

* * * * *

As Police Constable Donald Norton walked up the weed-free garden path between the shrub border on his right and the well-kept lawn on his left, the front door of the house was opened by Mrs Mavis Dudridge. Her steel-grey hair was as neat, if not neater than the miniature conifers on sentry duty either side of the porch. Her cheeks were flushed and her eyes red-rimmed and watery. She was wearing a check-patterned apron and wiping her hands in a matching tea-towel. PC Norton took off his helmet and followed her into the hallway.

She was obviously distressed so he skipped the formality of showing her his warrant card. He put his helmet on the hallway table and followed the lady of the house into her living room. The constable had just taken his notebook and pencil from the top pocket of his uniform when Mr Dudridge, wearing slippers and an old gardening coat, came in from the kitchen. 'Oh, Frank,' said Mavis, 'this is Constable Norton. He's come about the break-in.'

'It was a burglary, Mavis,' said Frank. 'It happened last night while we were asleep. It's housebreaking in the daytime, isn't it, Constable?'

'That's what we used to call it, Mr Dudridge, but the *1968 Theft Act, Section 9(1,2)* did away with the distinction. It's all *burglary* now even if nothing is actually stolen. Have you made your list of what's gone missing?'

'Mavis! Where did you put that list?'

'On the desk in your study, Frank. Hang on. I'll go and fetch it.'

'How did they get in, Sir?'

'They forced the back door. Follow me. You can see for yourself,' said Frank, leading the way into the kitchen. 'We'll need a new door and frame now. That'll bump up our insurance premiums.'

'Here you are, Constable,' said Mavis, joining them in the kitchen.

'Thank you, Madam,' said Donald, 'this will be very helpful.'

'What are your chances of catching these thieves, Constable?' asked Mavis.

Before Donald could reply, Frank turned to Mavis and said, 'You can kiss goodbye to that silver tea-service your Gran left you. They'll probably melt it down and turn it into tiny bits of metal for teenagers to stick through their nose and other places I don't care to mention.'

When Mavis started to cry, Donald decided it was time to leave. As he put on his helmet, he said to them, 'You might want to consider having an alarm system fitted.'

'Bit late for that. Closing the stable door now the horse has bolted,' retorted Frank.

'Actually it isn't,' said Donald. 'In the next month you are statistically twelve times more likely to be victims of another burglary than your neighbour who hasn't been burgled yet. You should get expert advice on making your home more secure.'

Donald closed the garden gate, put his bicycle clips around the bottom of his trouser legs and rode away in the direction of his married sister's house.

'What a nice young man,' said Mavis, drying her eyes. 'He got here pretty quickly.

'Waste of time,' said Frank. 'I'd better get on and sort out that kitchen door.'

'I'll make us a nice cup of tea first,' said Mavis. 'You fill in the claim form for the insurance before you start messing about in the kitchen.'

* * * * *

Broadstone had changed in the years since the first house of any size was built there in 1840. The railway line was long gone and the station, built in 1872, had been replaced by a fitness and leisure centre, complete with a 20-metre swimming pool. The population of the parish had increased to more than ten thousand souls and the number of crimes had risen accordingly. Donald cycled past all the banks, estate agents and shops in the busy main street, Lower Blandford Road, – still locally known as 'the village' – and headed downhill to the Derby's Corner roundabout and the local police station where he made out his report.

When he signed out at 4 o'clock he decided to drop in on Dorothy, his younger married sister, who lived with his brother-in-law, Ronald, just around the corner in the Waterloo Estate. His boots crunched on the weed-infested path as he walked to the kitchen door at the back of the house. His sister waved to him through the window as he leant his bike against the wall.

'Any chance of a cup of tea, Dot?'

'I put the kettle on as soon as I heard your big feet on the gravel drive. Sorry I can't offer you a chocolate biscuit. Ronnie had the last one last night and he hasn't given me this week's housekeeping money yet.'

'Still keeping you short, is he? What's he up to now?'

'He went to some meeting or other last week and came back all excited about how he's going to make us rich. He kept going on about MLM but I didn't pay much attention. When I said it sounded like a pyramid selling scheme, he got quite upset.'

'I can tell you, Dot, that multi-level marketing is definitely *not* the same thing as pyramid selling. MLM is a legitimate business operation that *could* make you a lot of money but it's not easy. I don't think it will suit Ronnie. It's too much like hard work. Speaking of work, when's he going to cut the grass?'

'You know Ronnie. He hates gardening. I'd suggest buying a goat to eat the grass and give us milk but he'd probably take me seriously and come up with another of his money-making schemes.'

'Where's the mower I gave him? He hasn't flogged it, has he?'

'No. It's in the shed. At least I think it is. I never go in there.'

'Right! Thanks for the tea,' said Donald, taking off his coat and rolling up his sleeves. I'll see if I can find that mower,'

Ronald Meeks appeared at the shed door just in time to watch Donald finish winding up the hover mower's electrical cable. The lawns, front and back, were now neatly cut and the mower was clean and oiled. Police Constable Norton didn't bother to point out to his brother-in-law that the lawns needed feeding and weeding. It would be a waste of breath. Instead, he asked him what he'd been up to lately. That was all Ronnie needed to launch enthusiastically into a detailed description of MLM and the wealth it promised.

'Did you know that multi-level marketing, or network marketing as it is now called, evolved over a 20-year period prior to the second world war? The biggest and longest established network marketing company operating worldwide is Amway - a contraction of the American way. In MLM you recruit people into your network and earn commission primarily from their sales and *not* from their recruitment or from selling them business support materials, etc. Network marketing is a legitimate operation and *not* a pyramid scam like a no-product scheme where recruits pay you money when they join and when they recruit others to join. And it's not the same as a product-based pyramid scheme where recruits may or may not pay you money to join but they buy your products for re-sale if they're lucky.'

'So what are you going to do, Ronnie? Become an Amway distributor?'

'Not likely. No, I'm going to start my own *bona fide* network marketing operation from scratch.'

'If you don't want me nicking you, Ronnie, make sure you're not starting a pyramid.'

'No chance of that. I won't charge people for joining and training – well not very much anyway. And we'll sell something. You know, we'll distribute a product. I just haven't decided what.'

'Just make sure you stay within the law. Oh, and by the way, give Dot her housekeeping.'

'You know me, Don. Honest Ron they call me. Thanks for mowing the lawns by the way.'

'That's alright. If you'd only feed and weed, they'd soon look like the lawn I saw this morning in West Way. Immaculate that was – just like the whole house.'

'What were you doing there?'

'An elderly couple were burgled last night. The thief or thieves got away with some family silver - the wife's grandmother's tea service. Worth quite a bit I imagine. Usual story. Poor locks, no bolts and no alarm system.'

'That's it!' said Ronnie.

'What? What is it?'

'My product,' said Ronnie. 'I'm going into the home security business. What was the number of that house in West Way?'

* * * * *

Mavis Dudridge was flattered that the owner of Watchdog Securities himself was calling personally to advise them just a week after the burglary. Ronald Meeks had polished his own shoes for once. Dorothy thought he was going down with something. He put on a clean white shirt, dark socks and his best suit and tie – actually his only suit and tie. Dorothy let him have her late father's black leather briefcase. He filled it with stationery he'd had printed and various catalogues he'd picked up locally. Dorothy straightened his tie, adjusted the lapels of his coat and sent the owner of Watchdog Securities out of the front door with a good luck kiss.

'It's so good of you to come personally, Mr Meeks,' said Mavis Dudridge.

'Think nothing of it, Mrs Dudridge. I felt it was the least I could do when Constable Norton happened to mention your misfortune. What dreadful times we live in. Who can you trust these days?' When Frank Dudridge came in from the kitchen, Ronnie leapt to his feet. 'Good morning, Sir. Mr Dudridge, is it?'

'That's right. I suppose you're the bloke come to sell us an alarm system we can't afford.'

'No, Frank,' said Mavis, 'that nice policeman told him we needed advice and Mr Meeks has come round personally to help us.'

'Quite right, Mrs Dudridge. No, Sir, I'm not a salesman. I own Watchdog Securities and we do supply alarm systems but I'm here just to offer some advice.'

'And what's this advice of yours going to cost me?'

'Frank! I do apologise for my husband, Mr Meeks. He can be a bit blunt.'

'No apology needed, Mrs Dudridge. I prefer a man who speaks his mind.'

'Would you join us in a cup of coffee?'

'Thank you, if that's not too much trouble. Not too strong. Milk but no sugar.'

While Mavis was in the kitchen Ronnie complimented Frank Dudridge on his front lawn and asked how he kept it so weed-free. That launched Frank into an account of the fertilisers and herbicides he used, including how and when he applied them. He had just started to describe his two different lawn mowers and the various heights of cut he used according to the time of year and the weather conditions, when Mavis came in with the coffee and a plate of biscuits. Ronnie made sure that Frank and Mavis had taken what they wanted before he selected a chocolate-covered orange cream wrapped in gold foil.

'I wish I had your green fingers, Mr Dudridge, I really do,' said Ronnie. 'My wife says I'm the angel of death when it comes to plants.'

'You just need time and patience, that's all. Mind you, it helps if you're retired. It wouldn't be the same if I were working full-time running a business like yours.'

'Now then, Mr Meeks, in your expert opinion, what should we do to make our little place more secure?' asked Mavis.

Ronnie had done his homework. He started with the obvious and the inexpensive. Put bolts on the outer doors and also a chain on the front door. Fit locks inside all ground floor windows. Then he moved on to the slightly more expensive.

Replace the spring tumbler lock on the front door with a minimum 1-inch deadbolt. Mount bright lights, activated by motion sensors, high on the walls at the front and back of the house. Replace the carriage lamp in the front porch by one activated by a motion sensor. Put a decoy/dummy bell box high up on the front of the house to fool thieves into thinking the house has an alarm.

And then, in response to Frank's question, Ronnie described the components of a full interior alarm system (control panel, infra-red motion detectors, magnetic door and window contacts, etc.) and discussed the pros and cons of installing wireless versus hard-wired systems.

When Ronnie walked down the garden path to the gate, he had a substantial order – the first of many - in his briefcase. Mavis and Frank Dudridge had persuaded him to take their order along with a second cup of coffee and another foil-wrapped chocolate biscuit. The first recruit into his network would be an old school pal, Tommy Fielding, who was a Do-It-Yourself enthusiast and a qualified electrician. Ronnie knew he'd never recruit his brother-in-law into his business but he planned to get his help.

PC Donald Norton called on Mr and Mrs Dudridge in the evening, the day after their alarm system had been installed and activated. As he opened the gate, a floodlight came on and nearly blinded him.

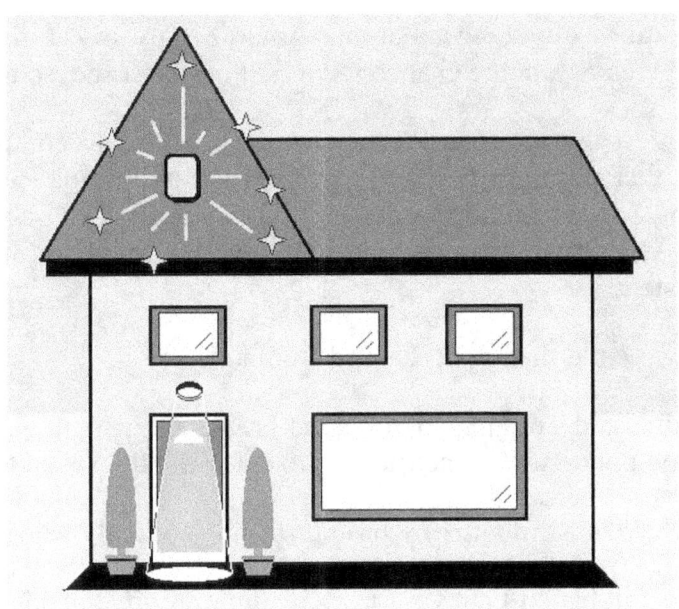

'Good evening, Mr Dudridge. Constable Norton, Sir.'

'Course you are,' said Frank. 'Everything alright, Constable?'

'Just passing by. I thought I'd check to see how you are. Looks like you've made your place more secure.'

'Yes, thanks to you,' said Mavis, who had come to the door. 'Watchdog Securities did a good job.'

'Cost a pretty penny,' said Frank, 'but we reckon it's worth it. Thanks again.'

* * * * *

Over the next twelve months Ronnie, and two more old school pals he recruited, visited homes recently burgled and listed as such in local neighbourhood watch bulletins. They offered a *Free Home Security Audit* and, as a result, usually took substantial orders for alarm systems that Tommy expertly fitted. Ronnie's most fruitful visits were always to homes that his police constable brother-in-law, Donald, had visited in response to the report of a burglary. Ronnie knew Donald never recommended his or any other security firm to the home owners. That didn't matter. What mattered was that

Ronnie knew about the burglary before any rival firm. The knowledge gave him the chance to be first on the scene, so to speak.

Ronnie soon registered his business as a private company. As Tommy the installer became more experienced and proficient, Watchdog Securities Ltd started to offer a wider range of alarms and services. One day Tommy suggested they should put in monitored alarm systems.

'How would that work?' asked Ronnie.

'Well,' said Tommy, 'if someone breaks in, a silent alarm goes off and the police will come running to catch the thieves in the act.'

'I'll have a word with my brother-in-law about it,' said Ronnie.

'You still haven't cut your lawn, Ronnie,' said Donald.

'Too busy. I've got a company to run.'

'Going well, is it?'

'Mustn't grumble. Anyway, if I did, nobody would listen. Look, Don, I need your help.'

'What is it this time? Want me to mow your lawn?'

'No, nothing like that. I want to pick your brains. How do we go about getting you blokes to monitor the alarm systems we're installing?'

'I haven't a clue. Getting a bit ambitious, aren't we?'

'Look, this is important. Can you look into this for me? We've been asked for a monitored system a couple of times now. Mustn't let our customers down.'

A few days later Donald cycled to his sister's house and left a note.

Ronnie,

The alarm should conform to the Association of Chief Police Officers (ACPO) Unified Intruder Alarm Policy. A remote signalling alarm should be hard-wired, maintained in accordance with an appropriate British Standard and, when registered with the police, identified by a Unique reference Number (URN). Watchdog Securities Ltd would be subject to inspection by independent organisations identified in the police policy.

You might want to tell your customers that the police may not respond if they have competing urgent calls or they are short staffed. If an alarm triggers a lot of false calls in a year, it will be given a lower police response priority.

Don

* * * * *

It looked as though Ronnie had found his niche. His marketing network never grew but Watchdog Securities Ltd was doing quite well. Ronnie made himself chairman. He made Dorothy secretary so she could claim her housekeeping as expenses. Tommy was treasurer. Ronnie's other two former school pals stayed as independent distributors and took a commission on sales.

Insomniac, their silent monitored alarm system, was beginning to worry their competition – the other local security firms. All would have been well if only Ronnie had not started reading some of these 'improve your small business' books. The 'Guru' who threw the spanner in Ronnie's works wrote, *No business stagnates – it either grows or it dies.*

The five members of Watchdog Securities sat around Dorothy's kitchen table, drinking her coffee and eating her biscuits. Ronnie called their informal meeting to order.

'We're stagnating,' said Ronnie. 'If we're not careful the business is going to die.'

'How do you make that out?' asked Tommy.

'We've had the same number of orders each month for the last three months,' said Ronnie.

'What's wrong with that?' chimed the two distributors in unison. 'Our orders are not going down.'

'That's not the point,' said Ronnie. 'They ought to be going up.'

'So what you're saying is,' said one distributor, 'we should be on the telephone cold calling or out there knocking on doors? *Good morning, madam, could I interest you in a security system? Oh, and by the way, we have a special on double glazing this month.*'

'If you want telephone cold calling, you can do it yourself,' said the other distributor.

'And I'm not knocking on doors at random,' said the first distributor.

'Unless the number of burglaries increases, Ronnie,' said Dorothy, 'you'll have to be content with the business as it is.'

'You've got a point there, my love. Meeting closed,' said Ronnie. 'Tommy! I'd like a word with you in private?'

* * * * *

Over the next six months, business picked up. Sales increased little by little. Watchdog Securities Ltd was no longer stagnating. It was growing. One afternoon, just before Donald was due to sign out, the station sergeant called him over to his desk. The sergeant wanted the opinion of the station's *neighbourhood watch liaison officer* on the small but steady increase in the number of local burglaries he had noticed in the station reports. According to the sergeant, two things didn't quite add up.

First of all, in most of the cases, there was very little damage and nothing was stolen. Second of all, this increase coincided with an increase in the number of neighbourhood watches being set up locally. Donald had to agree that it was curious but he could offer no explanation. Just as he turned to leave, the sergeant asked him if he'd investigated the recent noise complaint.

'Yes, Sarge. It was the major's trip flares going off late at night. I didn't file a formal report'

'Trip flares? What's all that about?'

PC Donald Norton explained.

'Some ex-army major strung a series of trip wires criss-crossing his rear garden backing onto what used to be the old railway line. He's been burgled three times in the past two months. They always came through the garden and used a jemmy on the kitchen door or window. First time the major's wife lost most of her jewellery. Second time they lost their silver dinner-service. Third time was the last straw. They took the major's medals and smashed his prize marrow.'

'So the thieves tried for a fourth time and set off these flares?'

'Hard to tell, Sarge. More likely it was a fox on the prowl. The neighbours got fed up being woken up in the middle of the night by all those loud bangs and flashes. I've had a word with the major. He didn't like it when I pointed out that he might be hounded by the Wildlife Protection Society or sued by a would-be burglar for damage to his ears and eyes. Anyway, I hung around until he'd turned his assault course back into a normal garden. The neighbours have probably heard the last thunderflash but not the last of the major.'

About two weeks later Donald was instructed to attend an evening meeting of a group of residents in the major's locality. It was not a gathering to complain about late night thunderflashes. The meeting was in the major's house to agree the formation of a neighbourhood watch. Donald attended in his capacity as neighbourhood watch liaison officer. It was almost a waste of his time. He handed out a leaflet but had little to say. The major was firmly in command and his night ops were clearly forgiven and forgotten.

The minutes of the meeting showed they unanimously agreed that (a) the major would be the new neighbourhood watch representative, (b) his telephone would receive from the police their recorded messages of local incidents and their alerts of criminal activities and (c) he would arrange through the local council to put an official sign on a nearby lamppost.

It was 10:55 p.m. when Donald put on his helmet and left the major's house to cycle home. A few minutes later he received on his two-way radio a message that a silent alarm had been activated in a house twenty yards down the road. He called back and informed the duty officer that he would investigate. Just before he reached the house, Donald switched off his front lamp and leant his bike quietly against the neighbour's garden wall. Then, torch in hand, he moved as quietly as his boots would allow to the house.

The front gate was open. Donald stepped onto the front lawn and crept up to the front door. He switched on his torch long enough to establish no sign of a forced entry there. Keeping to the lawn, he moved as quietly as possible to the rear of the house. It was in complete darkness. Just as he was about to shine his torch on the back door, he heard a faint sound from inside.

Somebody or something was moving around in the kitchen. The back door was open. He risked his torch again. The door was open. He tiptoed forward and stood alongside the door with his back to the wall. 'Patience is a virtue,' PC Donald Norton thought to himself. And sure enough, it was.

After a minute that seemed more like an hour, a figure crept out through the open kitchen door. 'Gotcha!' said Donald, grabbing the arm of the intruder's black tracksuit top. At 175lbs in weight and 6ft 3ins in height plus another 3ins of police helmet, PC Donald Norton's word was his command. 'Alright, my lad, let's take a look at you,' he said to his captive who was a mere 118lbs and 5ft 4ins tall. Donald shone his torch onto the intruder's face. 'What the...? Oh, Lord! What have you been up to?'

Donald quietly pushed the back door shut and without waking the occupants, left the property with the would-be burglar. With one large hand on the handlebars of his bicycle and the other firmly holding his captive's arm, he marched in the direction of the police station. When they reached Derby's Corner, he hesitated and then turned towards the Waterloo Estate. When they reached his sister's house, they went inside and sat down to face one another across the kitchen table.

'So,' said Donald, 'are you going to tell me what this is all about?'

'Watchdog Securities Ltd.'

'I might have guessed. How long has this been going on?'

'I'm not sure. Quite a while I suppose. I'm sorry. This must be a bit awkward for you.'

'You can say that again.'

'I really am sorry. It's just that the business wasn't growing and we thought...'

'You'd help it along.'

'Look, I never took anything and I did as little damage as possible. What happens now?'

'By rights I should arrest you and you'd be charged with burglary.'

'It wasn't my idea. You know that don't you?'

'Yes, I do. You'd never come up with such a hair-brained scheme yourself.'

'And you can guess why I did it, can't you?

'Yes, I can. You did it out of loyalty.'

'Well, yes that too I suppose. But really, I knew if he did it, he'd be caught the first night. I mean, he can't even mow a lawn.'

'Alright. Here's what I'll do. I'll report that there was no sign of an intruder when I arrived at the house and that the silent monitored alarm may have been set off by a cat.

'One of our competitor's alarms, was it?'

'No. As a matter of fact it was one of your own. Didn't Tommy tell you he'd installed it?

'No. But I usually don't know what's going on.'

'Anyway, I'm going to let you off with a caution but you must swear to me that tonight was your last attempted burglary.'

'I swear, Don. Never again.'

'Right, that's that then. I'd better be off. I've the early shift tomorrow,' he said heading for the door.

'Never again, Don. I promise.'

'Fine. Goodnight, Dot. Sleep tight.'

* * * * *

Epilogue

In 1982, the United Kingdom of Great Britain and Northern Ireland saw the launch of satellite TV, the start of the Falklands War and, in the sleepy village of Mollington near Chester, the formation of the first neighbourhood watch. One of the villagers brought back the idea from a visit to the USA and Canada. By 2007 there were more than 170,000 neighbourhood watch groups in the UK with over 10 million members.

The reduction in crime and increase in the sense of safety generated by the scheme underlines the value of knowing and getting on with your neighbours. I was instrumental in forming the neighbourhood watch in the cul-de-sac where we lived in Broadstone. I was our representative and our telephone received those recorded messages from the police. Our friendly neighbours referred to me as 'Colonel of the Watch.'

When we moved out of that cul-de-sac, we sold our house to, surprisingly enough, a real Colonel. He was only too willing to take command of our little neighbourhood watch. Shortly afterwards, my wife and I moved to Canada where, equally surprisingly, we have yet to be part of an official neighbourhood watch. I did try to form one but... well that is another story.

Keep reading for an excerpt from Michael C. Cox's novel

Once Upon A Term

available from Amazon in paperback and electronic book form

* * * * *

"The writing of solid, instructive stuff fortified by facts and figures is easy enough. There is no trouble in writing a scientific treatise on the folk-lore of Central China, or a statistical enquiry into the declining population of Prince Edward Island. But to write something out of one's own mind, worth reading for its own sake, is an arduous contrivance only to be achieved in fortunate moments, few and far in between. Personally, I would sooner have written Alice in Wonderland than the whole Encyclopaedia Britannica."

Stephen Leacock (Sunshine Sketches of a Little Town)

INTRODUCTION

"Truth is stranger than fiction, but it is because Fiction is obliged to stick to possibilities; Truth isn't." Mark Twain

* * * * *

This story is fiction but not pure and simple. Beaumont Abbey School does not exist. The activities of its staff and pupils are products of my imagination but not entirely so. In my experience of teaching in the independent, private sector, in England, facts have proved stranger than fictions. However, all the companies, events, organisations and places in this book are either the product of my imagination or used fictitiously.

The names and characters are figments of my imagination and any resemblance to actual persons, living or dead, is entirely coincidental. Now, should any former colleagues think I have included them in my story and, heaven forbid, portrayed them unfavourably, may I point out that more often than not the law seems to benefit the lawyers rather than the litigants.

* * * * *

Beaumont Abbey I imagine to have been founded by Sir Athelstan de Beaumont in 1587, during the reign of Elizabeth I, as a Public School, meaning, of course, a private school. I apologise to my friends in North America for the confusion. Some four hundred years or so later, I imagine the school is still private and independent of the state school system.

In my imagination, the school would be located on the border of the northern counties of Cumbria, Durham and Northumberland. Its ancient stone buildings would be listed to protect them from man but not the elements. Its modern buildings would contrast sharply.

The academic staff would be highly qualified, all men, individualistic and bordering upon the eccentric. Many, but not all, would themselves have been educated at an all-boys private boarding school. Their pupils would be sent to Beaumont, from the British Isles and other parts of the globe, to be similarly educated and become steeped in tradition.

The headmaster or principal - I call him the High Master – would be responsible to the board of governors and, in theory, overall in charge of the school. The deputy head or vice-principal – I call him the Second Master – would be responsible to the headmaster and, in practice, overall in charge of the school. The Housemasters would be members of the academic staff and responsible for the boys in their boarding houses.

The Bursar – often an ex-serviceman - would be responsible to the board of governors and in charge of the financial management of the school and the non-academic staff with, of course, the exception of the headmaster's secretary who is often a law unto herself.

This story concerns the third and final term in the academic year, the summer term - I call it the Trinity Term – in which the school is on the brink of becoming co-educational.

* * * * *

99

CHAPTER 1

"Childhood has no forebodings, but then, it is soothed by no memories of outlived sorrow." George Eliot - The Mill On The Floss

* * * * *

Dr Llywelyn Pugh-Jones gently tapped the shell of his soft-boiled egg in time with the music emanating from his radio, precisely and almost permanently tuned to the BBC Radio 3 Breakfast Hour programme. He sat alone in the kitchen. Louise, his wife, had taken her breakfast tray and Daily Telegraph newspaper into the relative peace and quiet of the sunroom. If she had broken her routine and stayed in the kitchen, perhaps the High Master of Beaumont Abbey might have paid attention more to his wife than to the music Sergei Prokofiev composed for the film *Lieutenant Kijé*. If she had eaten her breakfast at the kitchen table he might not have had two ideas, one of which nearly led to tragedy.

Reginald Thomas De Vere, MA (Cantab) covered the hot porridge with cold milk, added a sprinkling of granulated brown sugar, glanced at his wrist watch and began the Times crossword. Eighteen minutes and 23 seconds later he had finished the crossword but not the porridge. He poured himself a second cup of coffee from his *cafetière à piston* before selecting a croissant from the woven silver basket on the breakfast table. Reg, as he was fondly known to his colleagues, had been a widower for almost four years. His wife, Madeleine, whom he had met in Paris and who had been three years his junior when they wed, had died of a brain tumour when she had just turned fifty. She had given him the silver cafetière on their 25th wedding anniversary. He had given her the silver basket. They owned a small holiday cottage on the Dorset coast. All being well, Reggie, as his wife fondly called him, planned to retire there after four more years as Second Master at Beaumont Abbey.

Anthony Parker-Smythe, purportedly a former major in the Royal Army Pay Corps, had finished his porridge, his kipper, his cooked breakfast of two eggs, bacon, sausage and mushrooms and was halfway through his second slice of toast and marmalade when Elsie, his housekeeper came to clear the dining room table. His mouth was so full he could only nod in the direction of his china cup and saucer. She poured him some more coffee then disappeared before he could attempt a smile of gratitude, not that he ever smiled or was grateful. At the kitchen sink, Elsie began washing the dishes and resolving to hand in her notice at the end of the week. She had had enough of her employer, the Bursar of Beaumont Abbey, real name Tony Smith who, according to her late husband, had only risen to corporal in the Army Catering Corps.

Gregory Watson had, as usual, been for a 5k run, showered, shaved and changed into his gym kit and track suit before joining his wife, Kathy, and their two young children, Mark and Tracy, at the table for his bowl of cereal and glass of orange juice. He came to Beaumont Abbey straight from Loughborough University after gaining a joint honours degree in Geography and Sports Science and completing his teacher training. He was in his third year at Beaumont and expected to become Head of Physical Education when Walter Barnes retired at the end of the year. Greg looked forward to modernising the PE curriculum and Kathy looked forward to receiving more house-keeping money. Neither gave thought to the possibility of unforeseen difficulties.

Colin Harper overslept. It had been another disturbed night of bad dreams he might, with professional help, have erased from his mind. His colleagues in the Mathematics Department at Beaumont seemed not to notice or care about the dark rings around his puffy eyes and the bags underneath them. Had Dr Klaus Heilbronn, the Head of Maths, ever noticed or cared, he might have assumed his assistant, whom he had placed in charge of the computer room, was spending too much time staring too closely at too many screens. One strikingly good-looking boy not only noticed but also really cared.

Rupert Jardine had inherited his angelic good looks from his English mother, an actress of good repute, and his devilish ways from his American father, an entrepreneur of ill repute and head of a corporation specialising in computers and software engineering. He was flying business class from JFK airport to London, Heathrow where a chauffeured car would be waiting. He had mixed feelings about returning to Beaumont. Only two members of staff really liked him; the rest tolerated him. He knew he had overstepped the mark with his last prank; he was only being allowed back because the member of staff involved had not been seriously injured and because Randolph Jardine was a very wealthy man.

It was Saturday morning. The summer term was about to begin. At 10 o'clock sharp the staff of Beaumont Abbey would assemble in the Long Room for the High Master's words of welcome, for the

Second Master's notice of any changes affecting staff and for the Housemasters' lists of pupils flying in late from far flung regions of the globe or arriving on time but with a leg broken whilst skiing in the Alps. After the Chaplain's reminder that evensong in the chapel would begin at 7 p.m. on Sunday, the meeting would finish. The High Master would retreat to his study. The Second Master and staff would retreat to the Common Room for coffee or tea, biscuits and gossip. School would begin in earnest immediately after chapel on Monday morning. For most, the coming weeks would be hectic but normal. For a few, the summer term would be very hectic and not normal at all.

* * * * *

CHAPTER 2

"Meetings are indispensable when you don't want to do anything."
John Kenneth Galbraith – American Economist

* * * * *

He was deep in thought and chewing thoroughly the last fragment of his second piece of toast when his wife returned to the kitchen from the sun room.

'Good morning, Llew,' she said. 'How was your breakfast?'

'Fine, thank you Louise,' replied Dr Llywelyn Pugh-Jones, the High Master of Beaumont Abbey. 'Lacking in taste but healthy and nutritious. Just what my doctor ordered.'

'Not that bad, surely?' said Louise.

'Let me think for a moment. One half of a fresh grapefruit - *no sugar*. One soft-boiled egg - *no salt*. Two thin slices of *whole grain* toast - *no butter*. One small glass of orange juice – *unsweetened*. Oh, yes! *No coffee. No tea.*'

'Sounds delicious,' said Louise. 'In fact it was delicious. I had exactly the same.'

'Really? *Exactly* the same? No sugar on your grapefruit?'

'No! I did *not* sprinkle any sugar on my grapefruit,' Louise said haughtily, knowing her husband would not notice the pot of honey on her tray. 'Anyway, I'm not the one with a heart condition.'

There was a history of heart problems in the Pugh-Jones family. Llywelyn's grandfather was forty-six when he died. Llywelyn's father was forty-nine when he died. Both men had heart attacks. Both deaths were blamed on the men being overweight, heavy smokers and Welsh coal miners. Llywelyn believed he had already outlived his father by two years because he had never worked down a coal mine, he had never smoked and he was not overweight. At his last medical examination, the High Master of Beaumont weighed 174 pounds, stood 6ft 3in tall in his cotton socks and measured 35 inches around his waist. His body mass index (BMI) of 21.7 was exactly in the middle of the normal range. He felt he was in good physical shape for a man of his age but Louise made him go for a medical when he returned from a staff meeting complaining of a pain in his chest.

'Before you ask,' said Llywelyn, 'yes, I did take my blood pressure tablet. Thank you for putting it on my tray.'

'Will you be back here for lunch?'

'Hopefully but I must have a word with the Bursar after the staff meeting,'

'What's Nosey Parker been up to now?' said Louise. 'Nothing illegal, I trust.'

'You're not very fond of our Major Anthony Parker-Smythe, are you?'

'No, to be honest. Something not quite right about him. Too smarmy for words if you ask me,' said Louise.

'I think you're being a trifle harsh, my dear,' Llywelyn said, knowing full well his wife was a pretty good judge of character. 'The major knows how to handle Beaumont's finances.'

'Now *that* I don't doubt for one moment,' Louise said, with a wry look on her face.

* * * * *

The chapel, the walled garden and parts of the main building date back to 1587 when the school was founded by Sir Athelstan de Beaumont. Some of the trees in the extensive grounds are even older. The Long Room is actually more square than oblong. A little daylight filters through the narrow windows high above the tall oak panelling covering the walls but even when all the lights are switched on, the room remains gloomy. Ronald Beech, the head caretaker, was in the Long Room when the Second Master arrived.

'Good morning Mr De Vere.'

'Good morning Ron. Everything ready for the meeting?'

'Yes, sir,' said Ron. 'Tom and Dolly were in here first thing this morning. I just popped in to check they had finished. Tom buffed the floor while Dolly did the dusting.'

'How long have the Browns been with us now?' asked the Second Master.

'Must be going on for ten years now,' said Ron. 'Worth their weight in gold.'

'Yes indeed.'

'Tom will keep watch as usual,' said Ron. 'When he sees you leave the Long Room, he'll let Dolly know the meeting is over so she'll have the coffee in the Common Room for when the staff arrive. Now, if you'll excuse me, sir. I must be getting along.'

The door into the room was in the far corner of the shorter wall. Near the door and just inside the room, were two rectangular tables placed end to end and parallel to the shorter wall. Six more tables, in two sets of three, were placed end to end and parallel to the longer wall. The names of past pupils were carved on these eight heavy oak tables and bore witness to the age of the school.

On the two tables by the door was a green baize cloth, creating the illusion of one large table, and a silver tray bearing a jug of iced water and two glasses. Behind each half of the table, and close to the oak-panelled wall, was a chair with a carved high back and a padded seat. On the table in front of the chair furthest from the door, Reg placed the walnut gavel and block that had belonged to his great-grandfather. Dr Pugh-Jones mistakenly believed the Second Master's great-grandfather had been a judge. The Second Master was never afraid to correct the High Master when he was wrong but on this point he kept his own counsel. His great-grandfather had simply been an auctioneer. Reg glanced at his watch then strolled outside to await the arrival of the staff.

'Good morning, Second Master. Nice morning,' said Gregory Watson.

'Good morning, Greg. Been for our morning run, have we?

'Oh Yes. Too nice a day to stay in bed,' said Greg. 'Am I the first?'

'Only if you exclude me as a member of staff,' said Reg, with a smile.

'I stand corrected. I'm the second,' said Greg. 'If you'll excuse me, I'll go on in.'

Heavy oak chairs, with low backs and no padding, had been placed on either side of the long tables (two sets of three) running parallel to the longer walls of the room. These hard chairs were for the staff. There were, however, four high-backed, padded chairs, one either side and at the head of the long tables and nearest to the baize-covered table. These padded chairs were for the housemasters. Greg sat on the hard chair next to the padded chair nearest to the door because he wanted to be seen by the High Master and the Second Master. He also wanted to be first out of the door when the meeting ended.

It was three minutes to ten when Colin Harper came scurrying up the path.

'S-S-Sorry S-Second M-M-Master. Am I late?'

'No, Colin. You cut it fine. I see the High Master heading our way. Get inside before he sees you.'

'Yes. R-right. Th-Thank you, s-sir.'

'Good morning High Master,' said the Second Master. 'How are you this morning?'

'Fine! Never felt better,' said Dr Pugh-Jones. 'All present and correct?'

'Yes. Everyone is here.'

'Good. Let's get started. Lead the way.'

* * * * *

When the Second Master entered the room, the staff stood up. Then the High Master entered the room and took his seat behind the baize-covered table. When the Second Master had taken his seat alongside the High Master, the staff sat down. The Second Master poured two glasses of iced water and placed one in front of the High Master. Even though the only sound in the room was the ice tinkling against the sides of the High Master's glass as he sipped his water, the Second Master struck the walnut block three times with his walnut gavel. It was exactly ten o'clock. The High Master cleared his throat.

'Good morning, gentlemen. Welcome back to Beaumont Abbey. I hope you all enjoyed your Easter break and are ready for the Trinity term. I am sure I need not remind you that the first half is a crucial time for the Upper Fives and Upper Sixes. Good examination results are not of course the be-all and end-all - *pause for a sip of water* – but at this time in a boy's life they will decide what options he may have for his future. It is up to us to see that every boy gives of his best. Beaumont has built up a reputation for academic excellence that should be reflected in the examination results. The future of the school may depend on them. I, as do the boys, put my trust in all of you. Thank you.'

As the High Master turned to leave, all the staff (except Geoffrey Rusbridge who was engrossed in the Financial Times) stood up and stayed standing until he had left the room and closed the door behind him. The Second Master sat down, drank some iced water and used his gavel again. David Peters stood up and said the delay of a flight from Singapore would mean five boys from Armstrong house might not be back in time for Sunday evensong. Some younger members of staff seated at the back of the Long Room sniggered when they heard the Housemaster read out the names in rapid succession: Chin, Chin, Kung, Fu and Woo.

The Second Master managed to keep a straight face and called upon the Housemaster of Burdett. Ralph Abrahams leaned forward out of his seat, said he had nothing to report and sat back down. Alan Radford reported for Gower that Morris Minor might be late. Before he could explain, someone at the back of the room whispered audibly *engine trouble* and caused more sniggering. The Second Master used his gavel. The Housemaster of Gower then explained the boy was recovering from influenza.

'Wedgewood,' said the Second Master, looking at E. Gordon Hamilton.

'Thank you, Second Master,' said Hamilton rising slowly to his feet, blithely unaware of the restless shuffling of some feet at the back of the room. 'I have six boys delayed on the same flight to which Mr Peters referred.'

'The flight from Singapore?' said the Second Master.

'Yes!' said Hamilton, a modern linguist.

'Your Chinese contingent?'

'Yes!' said Hamilton.

'How's their English coming along?'

'They speak English almost as well as they speak Cantonese and Mandarin,' Hamilton said somewhat tetchily. 'May I read out their names?'

'Yes, of course,' said the Second Master.

'Chén, Chéng, Liú, Wáng, Yáng and Zháng.'

'Thank you Mr Hamilton,' said the Second Master. 'Since some of us do not have your ear for the four tones of Chinese - the first two sounded the same to me - would you spell those names.'

'If you wish,' said Hamilton, again ignoring more restless shuffling of feet. After he had spelled each name carefully, including the accents over the vowels, he remained standing.

'Do you have anything else, Housemaster?' asked the Second Master.

'Just one question, if I may,' said Hamilton. 'What has the High Master decided to do about Jardine?' No more shuffling of feet or nervous coughing. The room was silent.

'He is being allowed back to complete his year in the Lower Sixth. No decision has yet been made about his continuing into the Upper Sixth.' The murmurs around the room masked Colin Harper's sigh of relief at the news.

'When, may I ask, were we to be informed of this decision?'

'Today. Mary Cranborne sent a note to you, and the Heads of Maths and Physics, for a meeting with the High Master and myself this afternoon at 2 p.m.'

'Will Jardine still be denied privileges, Second Master?' asked Gregory Watson.

'That's something we shall be discussing this afternoon. We'll try not to deny the First Eleven its opening fast bowler.'

The Second Master looked around the room, glanced at his watch, picked up his walnut gavel and said, 'Coffee awaits us in the Common Room. Is there any other business, gentlemen?' No hand was raised and heads were shaking, so he struck the walnut block a resounding blow and declared the meeting closed.

* * * * *

Dr Llywelyn Pugh-Jones closed the Long Room door quietly and walked slowly from the portico out into the sunshine, unbroken by the few wispy clouds in a pale blue sky. Directly ahead of him was a concrete path leading straight to the main building and the Bursar's office. To his right was a gravel path, bordered on both sides by well-tended beds of assorted evergreen flowering shrubs – azaleas, japonica, rhododendrons, skimmia and viburnum – that would lead him first to the walled garden. He hesitated just for a moment then turned right onto the gravel path.

His doctor advised a brisk walk every morning. Llywelyn was a good patient and usually took his doctor's advice but not this morning. He was in no hurry to see Nosey Parker, as his wife Louise called the Bursar, Anthony Parker-Smyth. Llywelyn pretended he was just out for a stroll. It was after all a beautiful morning. He savoured the fragrant scent from the tiny white flowers of the skimmia and viburnum and feasted his eyes upon the purples and reds of the azaleas and rhododendrons. A thrush, hiding in the shrubbery, suddenly stopped its flutelike song when it heard Llywelyn's footsteps on the gravel path.

Perhaps the birdsong reminded him of the music on the radio that morning. Llywelyn began to hum Prokovief's sleigh ride tune, Troika, and to recall that in a short story by Vladimir Dal and published in 1870, Kijé was an imaginary officer brought into being by a bureaucratic blunder. Emperor Paul I of Russia promotes Kijé to lieutenant, captain and eventually to colonel. When the Emperor asks to see the colonel and the bureaucrats realise their original blunder will be discovered, they inform the Emperor that Colonel Kijé has died. The whimsical thought, of bureaucracy creating an imaginary person that the authorities treat as a real person, was going through his head when he arrived at the Bursar's office. Dr Pugh-Jones smoothed his thinning ginger hair, tousled during his stroll, drew himself up to his full height, knocked once and strode briskly into the room.

'Ah, High Master! Good morning, sir,' said Nosey, putting down his coffee cup and rising to his feet. 'Beautiful morning! You're looking extremely well this morning, if I may say so. How is Mrs Pugh-Jones these days?'

'She is very well. Thank you for asking, Anthony.'

'May I offer you some coffee?' said Nosey, reaching for the jug on the tray on his desk.

'I should refuse, doctor's orders and all that, but on this occasion I *will* say yes to a small cup,' said Llywelyn. 'Milk but no sugar if you please.' Having committed this minor transgression, he sat down and, while his coffee was being poured and he was attempting to prepare his opening remarks, he noticed Nosey also poured himself a whole cup of coffee and added two spoonfuls of brown sugar and a generous helping of full cream.

'Here you are, High Master,' said Nosey, reaching across his large mahogany desk to hand Llywelyn his half cup of coffee. 'I hope you like it. It's made from the *arabica* bean. They're a bit more expensive than the *robusta* bean but the coffee is more aromatic, has more flavour but only half the caffeine of coffee made from robusta beans.

'Only half the caffeine, you say? Very interesting.'

'May I offer you a chocolate biscuit?' said Nosey.

'Thank you, no,' said Llywelyn. 'Not good for the cholesterol and lipids in the blood, so I'm told.'

'Actually,' said Nosey, 'these are Belgian biscuits. Thin wafer coated in dark chocolate which, I am told, is good for you. Please try one.'

'Oh, very well. Just one. Thank you.'

The two men sat facing one another in silence, a silence broken only in their heads by the crunching of a chocolate biscuit and the swallowing of arabica coffee. His secretary, Mrs Susan Taylor, had reminded the Bursar that the High Master would be dropping in but had been unable to tell him the reason for his visit. Nothing in his visitor's manner so far led Nosey to believe he had anything to be nervous about. He kept calm and tried not to think about accounts and financial records. The High Master had instructed his secretary, Mary Cranborne, to tell the Bursar he would come to see him on Saturday morning straight from the Long Room. When Mary wanted to know the purpose of his visit in case Susan asked, Llywelyn told her to say it was just to say hello. 'No, Sue,' said Mary, 'Dr Pugh-Jones didn't say why he'll be dropping in. Probably just wants to chat. Nothing serious. Nothing specific.' But of course Mary Cranborne, BA. had worked for the High Master long enough to know that he would never chat, that he was always serious and that he would have something quite specific in mind.

'You wanted to see me, High Master?' said Nosey, breaking the silence.

'Yes, Anthony,' said Llywelyn. 'It's about money, I'm afraid.

* * * * *

FACTS AND FANTASIES – Volume 1

1. The lawn

This story is a fiction based upon facts personally reported to me and upon events I experienced firsthand. For instance, I knew a chemist, who left a major chemical company, solved a pollution problem, published a book of walks to unusual places, brewed his own wine and who, inspired by the fall of a cast iron gutter that might have killed his son, made his fortune in PVC guttering and downpipes.

2. The Axeman cometh

On the 12th of December 1966, Frank Mitchell absconded from Her Majesty's prison high on Dartmoor in the English county of Devon. The following story is true and as accurate as my memory permits. I have not changed the names of the people involved, so I apologise in advance to those (living or dead) mentioned herein who might feel that I have portrayed them in a worse light than I portrayed myself.

3. A tick in a Box

A Canadian source defines bureaucracy as a hierarchy of authority and a system of rules, regulations and record keeping characterized by division of labour and specialization of functions. A British source defines bureaucracy as an excessively complicated administrative procedure. After reading this story, the reader will, I trust, take more care than I did when completing any official form but heed the words of Robert Frost, "If we couldn't laugh, we would all go insane."

4. The journey of a canvas bag

Air is a liquid at minus 200 degrees centigrade. In their research at Bristol University, chemistry students often needed liquid air for their experiments. They kept the liquid in open-necked vacuum flasks to slow its evaporation. This story is based upon an incident that actually took place on a train travelling from Bristol to Southampton around 1958-59. Apart from Bob, all the characters are figments of my imagination. Two of the characters appear in the first story in volume 2 of my collected short stories.

FACTS AND FANTASIES – Volume 2

1. The best laid schemes

My parents, like many people after World War II, did not have a car. I was fortunate. John, a friend of mine, taught me to drive his small Morris Oxford which he used for work. He was a travelling door-to-door brush salesman. John liked some of the people he met but disliked the job, so he eventually went back to work for an insurance company. He disliked that work rather less but some of his co-workers rather more. The idea for this story stems from my recollection of John's account of life as a salesman and an insurance clerk.

2. What are the chances?

Certain people and chance events change our lives. They make us reconsider our beliefs, discard our old habits and gain a new sense of purpose and direction. This true story is about my father and an event that achieved quite the opposite. It gives credence to the adage 'Old habits die hard' and, dare I say it, to the adage 'You can't teach an old dog new tricks.' In regard to the first, I fear that I follow in my father's footsteps.

3. A mixed blessing

This story is a confession of a crime I committed out of false pride and in a moment of weakness more than forty years ago. By now both the statute of limitations and the statute of repose have probably run out and the long arm of the law in England is unlikely to reach across the Atlantic Ocean to Canada but, to be on the safe side, I ask you to believe the name of my victim and the associated geographical details to be pure fiction.

4. The lawnmower

This is a true story. By that I mean I have described a real incident to the best of my ability and memory. However, I have not disclosed the names of the real people involved. Any former friends and neighbours who think they recognise themselves and take exception to being excluded or included will, I trust, accept my apologies and neither strike me from their Christmas card list nor add me to their to-be-sued list.

FACTS AND FANTASIES – Volume 3

1. Deception and a deadly switch

The truth underlying this story is the foolish unsecured loans that two colleagues and I made to a former colleague and his brother in 1991. The name of the school, the names of the two companies and the names of the characters, apart from my own, are fictitious. I definitely lost money. I believe I was deceived. I think it best not to comment further.

2. A gorilla in the cupboard

This story concerns a real event I witnessed and a likely consequence I imagined. I have not named the school where this occurred or used the real names of the teachers and pupil concerned in order, hopefully, to avoid costly legal actions. To any former colleagues who were also witness to the event and who might think themselves unfavourably portrayed in my story, may I assert that the names and characters are the product of my imagination and any resemblance to actual persons, living or dead, is entirely coincidental.

3. Water of life

The Bristol-Bordeaux family-to-family exchange began in 1947 with one teacher and twenty-seven pupils from Fairfield Grammar School. The scheme rapidly expanded. In the Easter of 1951, more schools – my own included – were involved and more than one hundred pupils took part - myself included – even though I was no longer studying French. In April 2007, the exchange scheme celebrated its 60th year jubilee.

4. What the eye does not see

My wife and I once owned some timeshare at Castillo Beach Club, a resort on the lower slope of a hill overlooking Caleta de Fuste on Fuerteventura in the Canary Islands. The reception, bar and restaurant were in the main area known as Lake. The other area, known as Moon, was on the other side of the Calle de Virgen de Guadalupe. There are still squirrels on Chipmunk Hill. The supermarket (El Supermercado) and restaurant (El Papagayo) may still operate. I am not sure. The characters and events in this story are pure fantasy but the settings are real enough.

www.ingramcontent.com/pod-product-compliance
Lightning Source LLC
Chambersburg PA
CBHW070455130626
46555CB00003B/1009